STAGE LINE TO RINCON

NE TO
RINCON

Clement Hardin

Chivers Press
Bath, England

Thorndike Press
Waterville, Maine USA

This Large Print edition is published by Chivers Press, England, and by Thorndike Press, USA.

Published in 2002 in the U.K. by arrangement with the author c/o Golden West Literary Agency.

Published in 2002 in the U.S. by arrangement with Golden West Literary Agency.

U.K. Hardcover ISBN 0–7540–4935–3 (Chivers Large Print)
U.K. Softcover ISBN 0–7540–4936–1 (Camden Large Print)
U.S. Softcover ISBN 0–7862–4188–8 (Nightingale Series Edition)

The text of this Large Print edition is unabridged.
Other aspects of the book may vary from the original edition.

Set in 16 pt. New Times Roman.

Printed in Great Britain on acid-free paper.

British Library Cataloguing in Publication Data available

Library of Congress Cataloging-in-Publication Data

Hardin, Clement, 1916–
Stage line to Rincon / Clement Hardin.
p. cm.
ISBN 0–7862–4188–8 (lg. print : sc : alk. paper)
1. Coaching—Fiction. 2. Colorado—Fiction.
I. Title.
PR3527.E9178 S73 2002
813'.54—dc21 2002020713

CHAPTER ONE

Afterward Travis Holman thought he might have heard three separate gunshots, but they came so close together—the echoes so battered and scrambled by these rugged, rock-and-pine hills—that he wasn't completely sure. He couldn't even have said if they came from a rifle or a handgun, or whether from one or several weapons. Pulled up sharply in the saddle, he sat with head canted, listening, after the rolling sounds were swallowed up and silenced.

He let his shoulders fall, with the release of trapped breath, and shoved back the rifle he had slid halfway from its scabbard under his knee.

A man of perhaps medium height, this Travis Holman had a way of carrying himself, on the ground or in the saddle, that made him look bigger. Despite a tough beard he kept his jaws clean shaven, except for a tawny mustache that half concealed a long-lipped and sensitive mouth. The gray eyes somehow gave the impression they had seen a shade too much. The skirt of a brown corduroy coat, thrown back, showed the efficient leather holster and the polished cherry grips of the gun he wore strapped at his waist, and the faint glint of extra brass in the belt's loops.

The shots seemed to have been placed somewhere ahead. In this jumble of granite hills and pine forest, it would have been hard to say. But he had them in mind as he booted the dun horse and sent him on through shifting sunlight and shadows with the resinous scent of the pines heavy about him and the stillness that was broken, now, only by a brushing of wind through the branches and by the sound of his own passage.

Abruptly the stage road he followed dropped away into a shallow canyon, with a rocky stream boiling at the bottom. Between the stream and the lift of broken wall that climbed into timber he at once saw the stagecoach and its four-horse teams standing motionless, facing in his direction and foreshortened by the height from which he viewed them. He checked the dun and stared down at them with narrowed eyes.

Both doors of the coach stood wide open. There was no driver on the seat, no movement except for the horses stamping impatiently and shaking their harness. It was all very wrong; caution beat high in Holman as he spoke to the dun and sent it down the road which had been partially dug out of solid rock.

With the white water stream frothing and leaping close by to cover other sounds, he came on toward the stalled coach, noting now the lettering painted above the door: RINCON EXPRESS. The team caught his horse's scent and moved around a little in the traces, and for the first time Holman caught sight, between their legs, of the figure of a man lying motionless on the ground and another kneeling over him, apparently trying to stanch a copious flow of blood. He was too absorbed in his work, and the creek made too much racket for him to be aware of a newcomer until the horse and rider were almost upon him. Then he jerked up quickly, and Holman saw a face that was deeply scored by time and weather: a beak of a nose and fierce blue eyes, beneath sparse white hair which the canyon breeze stirred about his scalp. His stare was hostile and suspicious. Had he owned a gun Holman suspected he would have pulled it; but apparently he was unarmed.

'What happened here?' Holman demanded.

A stare that was infinitely bitter met his own. 'What does it look like?'

Not bothering to answer immediately, Holman dismounted. The hurt man was still alive, as the shallow rise and fall of his chest showed. But he had been shot at least twice, through shoulder and leg, and the leg wound had bled badly. The old fellow had been working on it with strips torn from the wounded man's shirt, and he seemed to have a tourniquet functioning to check the flow. But it was no better than a makeshift.

'He's in a bad way,' Holman observed.

'He's gonna die,' the old man said darkly.

'There's a bullet still in his chest, and the one that drilled his leg must have cut an artery. The damn fool! Even if he did hire to ride shotgun, he had orders not to take chances against odds like those!' His voice broke from grief, plainly for the loss of a friend.

From the man's hands—turned to hard clubs of callus and scar tissue from the years of handling leather—Holman would have known without being told that he was the driver. There was a tracery of blood and a swelling knot in the thinning hair above one ear, and Holman said, 'You didn't come through without a mark yourself.'

The other shrugged. 'I kind of lost my head, I guess, when they shot Len McCabe. I tried to grab the carbine before it could slide off his lap, and one of the bastards rode up close and clipped me with his gun barrel, stunned me good.' He touched the place and winced. 'They collected McCabe's weapons and thrun 'em into the creek, yonder. Then they took what they wanted and rode off.' He gestured to a brush-choked draw that broke the stretch of rock and scrub which rose above them. Holman would have guessed the attackers had made use of this in their surprise attack and getaway.

'What were they after?' he asked, and got a stabbing look.

'What the hell do you reckon? Gold bullion, of course—from the Princess mine down at

Rincon.' The old man spat into the dirt. 'I've drove for some hard luck outfits in my time, but this Rincon Express carries the biggest jinx I ever met up with. A half dozen shipments they've lifted off this line, in the past four months!'

Holman's lips shaped a soundless whistle. 'That's a poor record.'

'It's the most held up freight and stage line in the state of Colorado! The Princess ships a treasure box every fortnight by one of our coaches or freight wagons, and no matter how we try shifting things around, somehow the damned road agents never seem to miss hitting the right ones. God knows how they manage.'

'You're sure they're always the same outfit?'

The old man shrugged again. 'They don't wear name tags, they wear masks. The way they work, though, it has to be the same . . .' He broke off, his tone taking on a different edge, as he said, 'But I'm damned if I know why I'm telling all this to a stranger—or what makes you so interested!'

'It's no time for questions,' Holman agreed. 'This man has got to have a doctor if he's going to make it at all.'

'It's a good piece back to Rincon. I'll get him there.'

'What about yourself?'

'A little headache won't stop Burl Dempster!' The old fellow surged to his feet, and then had to put a hand on a big wheel of the coach to steady himself. But his voice was firm enough. 'Maybe you'd give me a hand putting him aboard. I'll get this rig turned around, and—'

'No!'

They both glanced up, Travis Holman in considerable surprise. He hadn't known the coach held a passenger. The woman might have been huddled in a corner of the seat all this time in a state of shock and fright from the violence of the holdup and the shooting of the guard. Her face was still white as she bent to look out at them, clutching the frame at either side of the open door and with one buttoned shoe on the iron step, visible beneath the hem of a bottle green traveling skirt. Rich auburn hair had come undone to hang in wings at either side of a delicately molded face; her eyes were dark stains, wide in consternation.

She said again, 'No! We can't go back!'

'Sorry, ma'am.' He had seen the thin gold band on her left hand, white knuckled as it clutched the doorframe. 'Don't look like there's much choice.'

'But I have a ticket to Seven Pines. And this coach is on a schedule.'

'The hell with the schedule,' the driver said. 'Your ticket will be honored another time, Miz Sorenson.'

Her handsome face twisted tight. Emotion put a tense line about her mouth. 'I *insist* we go on! You just don't understand. It's impossible for me to go back! There are reasons . . .' Then, as she saw her pleas were useless, her mouth began to tremble. The tears spilled over, and she was weeping with angry frustration and some other inner turmoil that Travis Holman could only guess at.

Looking at her, he wondered at the private trouble she had thought, perhaps, to leave behind her in the town of Rincon. He could almost have felt sorry for her.

But he said again, crisply, 'I'm sorry. A man's life is in the balance. Don't you understand?' Not wasting any more time on her, he turned again to the driver. 'Let's load him in.'

They laid hold and raised the hurt man, gingerly. Then, as Burl Dempster held him propped against the bottom of the door, Holman climbed inside. Between them they maneuvered him onto the forward seat, fitting him as well as possible into a space that was really too small for him to lie prone. Once, a groan was torn from Len McCabe and Holman thought he was going to recover consciousness; but he went limp again.

The effect on the woman, though, was startling. She cried out, tried to bolt and was almost out of the coach when Holman caught and hauled her back. At once she turned on him, striking with her fists, attempting to tear loose. He saw wild panic in her eyes. Simply and efficiently he struck her in the face with his open palm, and she subsided at once.

Pressed back against the seat, she stared at him. Her tongue came out and wet her lips. The print of his fingers was stark against the color slowly returning to her cheeks. She said in a muffled tone, 'I'm terrified of blood!'

'A lot of people are,' he said, trying to steady her with the sound of his voice. 'But I'm afraid right now you're going to have to help us.'

She swallowed. 'What do you mean?'

'This is a tourniquet,' Holman explained, showing her the binding Dempster had improvised from a strip of cloth. 'It's to keep him from bleeding to death, but it will have to be loosened every fifteen minutes or so to allow for circulation. You do it by twisting this stick. I'll show you.'

Her eyes never left his face. They became rounder and brightened with horror. 'I?' Revulsion twisted her mouth. 'I won't touch him!'

'Somebody has to do it. And I'm afraid you're elected.'

'Why not you?'

Holman shook his head. 'I'll not be going with you,' he answered crisply. Not waiting for further protests, he backed out of the coach and dropped to the ground, closing the door on her and the hurt man.

Burl Dempster had already climbed to the box and was collecting the leathers. Holman saw him squint and make a grimace of pain.

'Are you sure you can manage?'

'Hell, yes.' But then the old man reached into a hip pocket and dug out a bandanna handkerchief which he tossed down. 'Could you wring that out in the crick for me?' Quickly, Holman went across the road, scrambled down to the water's edge and dipped the cloth into icy water. When he brought it back and passed it up, the old man held the wet cloth to his head a moment, then knotted it about his temples. He had found his hat—a sweaty, shapeless wreck with an eagle feather stuck in the band—and he gingerly placed this atop the makeshift bandage.

Looking down at the stranger then, with the reins ready in his bands, he said gruffly, 'I appreciate your help, mister. But now I'm gonna have to stretch this team out if I'm to do Len McCabe any good and you likely won't want to keep up with us. Maybe I'll be seeing you in Rincon?'

'Could be,' Holman said. And then, as the man gave his attention to his horses, he added, 'How many would you say there were in the gang that hit you?'

The question made the driver's head come around, his scowl settling on the other again. 'Four that I seen,' he answered carefully. 'Why?'

Holman glanced toward the draw leading to higher country. 'Somebody ought to take a look at that trail while it's fresh. Could save valuable time later, for a sheriff's posse.'

'There'll be no posse,' Dempster told him. 'Sheriff's office is eighty miles away, and his deputy at Rincon can always think of some reason not to get up off his lazy butt. If *they* ain't concerned, why should you be?'

'Just the same,' the other answered, 'I think I'll have a look.'

Burl Dempster was staring at him, leaning forward on the high seat. Suddenly he exploded. 'Mister, you been holding something back? *Just who the hell are you?*' Holman, however, ignored the question. He turned toward his dun, which had stood waiting patiently, and heard Burl Dempster swear under his breath. A moment later the brake was kicked off and the stage teams were yelled into motion.

It was a bad place for a turnaround. Pausing to watch, Holman expected to see the horses tangle in their harness as the gnarled hands on the reins pulled them sharply over, causing them to shoulder one another in a kind of dancing sidestep. The coach cramped its wheels and, for a moment, tilted sharply as one broad tire threatened to slip over the edge toward the tumbling creek below.

But the old man was an expert. Having made the turn safely, he slapped the leathers against his horses' rumps, and the ferocious yells that spilled from his throat got them stretched out into a lunging start—almost as though he meant to run them all the way to Rincon. Travis Holman had a last glimpse through the window of the red-haired woman pressed back into her corner as though trying to withdraw as far as possible from the bloody shape that shared the coach with her.

A turn hid stage and horses. The sounds faded and the dust settled; he was alone with the busy, brawling voice of the creek that rushed through the throat of the canyon.

CHAPTER TWO

The draw was narrow and steep, and the raiders had taken it single file, both in coming and going. Thus although there were plenty of tracks, they were too jumbled and confused to make much out of them. Four riders, the old stage driver had said. But after climbing a little distance Holman reached a point where from the sign another horseman seemed to have waited for them.

Moments later he revised this guess. Marks of the tie rope were plain, showing that they had left that fifth animal tied in scrub growth that clung to the broken rock—a pack animal, then. That made good sense. After transferring the heavy treasure box to its back, they would have had easier going than with one of their number trying to balance it across his saddle.

Holman listened to the stillness, complete here except for the faint movement of the wind pushing through scrub growth. He could see only a few yards ahead. Fingering the backstrap of his holstered gun, be had to consider whether he wanted to risk blundering into an ambush in country he knew nothing about. But then, with a fatalistic shrug, he ticked the dun with a spur and sent it on up the draw.

Presently the draw played out. He crossed a rocky shoulder and came out upon a broad saddle between a couple of barren granite peaks whose heads were wreathed in cloud. The floor of the saddle held scatterings and clumps of pine, dark green against the drab gray rock. The sign crossed this, threading through the timber and making toward higher ground on the saddle's north edge.

He could make better time here but he still went cautiously. Once he reined up, reaching for his gun, at a sudden disturbance to his left; he caught himself when he sighted a doe bounding off across the high meadow to disappear in farther timber. Rueful over the state of his own nerves, he kicked the dun ahead.

There was considerable down timber among the standing pines, flattened by wind or by heavy winter snow; they lay about him like tangled jackstraws, silvered by time and weather. As he rode through the trees, he heard a faint rumble of thunder in the pile up of clouds gathered dark about the shoulder of the peaks.

Beyond the trees the trail began to climb again, over loose rubble that made the dun scramble for footing. And at that moment, while Holman was busy with the horse, a rifle shot lashed upon the stillness.

A bullet stamped into the earth not a yard from him, raising a quick eruption of rock chips. His involuntary jerk on the reins, and the dun's own fright, set the animal rearing. It lost its footing briefly, whickering in fear and going to its knees before it could scramble up again. Echoes of the shot were rolling away in fading pulsations, battered among the peaks, as Holman cursed and fought the horse around. After that, he had it speeding back into the shelter of the trees. A second shot followed them in.

Immediately Holman was leaping down, whipping the rifle from his saddle as he dropped. The horse ran on, and he threw himself into cover behind a decaying log. High up the face of the hill that formed the north side of the saddle, a spurt of white powder smoke was just melting against the tumble of rocks where the rifle—only one, apparently—was hidden. Face grim, Holman knelt and shouldered the stock of his saddle weapon and threw off three shots as fast as he could.

The moment his rifle fell silent there was an answer from the weapon in the rocks. The bullet was lost somewhere but it served its purpose. It showed Holman that the rear guard the stage robbers had left had picked a nearly impregnable position and was prepared to defend it. His rifle held a commanding view of the saddle below him. To approach or to go around him, both seemed equally unlikely.

As he debated, Travis Holman looked toward his dun horse, standing under the flickering tree shadows, and what he saw made him swear. Quitting his place, he took a closer look. Sure enough, the dun stood on three legs, its near forefoot lifted. Examining the hoof showed nothing, but when he took the reins and led the animal for a few steps it came reluctantly, limping.

There could be no doubt of it. The leg had been twisted in that tumble.

Holman stood with a hand on the dun's shoulder, while he looked off through the trees toward the hole up in the rocks where the man with the rifle was still waiting, no doubt to *see* what he would do. But there was nothing he could do with his horse going lame. No chance of going ahead; he would be lucky not to end up being set completely afoot, a dozen miles from anywhere.

Disgusted with the turn of events, he shoved the rifle back into the boot and knelt for a closer look at the foreleg.

* * *

It took time and patience, but working on the leg, alternately walking and riding and with long delays while he rested the dun to prevent it from completely giving out, he finally made his destination. When he came in at last toward the lights that must mark the town of Rincon, dusk was settling toward full darkness. And Travis Holman, who had walked much of the distance on a handful of jerky from his saddlebag, was footsore, bone weary and hungry.

He could judge very little about the town itself in this first view of it. One came upon it almost by surprise: tucked away in this remote part of the San Juans, in a sheltered pocket, a park almost, ringed by the high peaks. Mellow squares of lamplight marked out the general pattern of scattered buildings ranged along crisscrossed streets; other, more distant lights must indicate the workings of the Princess mine, at the edge of hills surrounding the park. Sulfur stink from the smelter laced the piney night breeze and caused Holman to grimace in distaste. Perhaps people here were used to the smells, he thought.

The twin ruts of the stage road brought him in over the rolling acres of the park and on a plank bridge across the burbling meadow creek, where he stopped to let his horse have a drink while the first stars began to dot the deepening sky and float, reflected on the sliding water. Holman was thinking mostly of food for himself and his horse, a stall for the dun and a bed for himself. But at the edge of the town he came upon a sprawl of buildings and corrals and a high fence with the shapes of freight wagons silhouetted above it. Horses stirred in the corrals, and he heard the braying of a mule from the direction of a row of dark stock sheds. Letters painted on the glass of a lighted window in the small office building spelled the name of the *Rincon Express and Freight Co.—Frank Chess, Prop.*

Drawing rein, he looked at that window for a moment and then rode over to the open gate in the wagon yard fence, drawn by a spot of light close to the trampled and barren earth. It proved to be an oil lantern, set on the ground to give light for a workman tinkering with the underpinnings of a wagon, while a second man stood by with hands thrust in hip pockets, obviously supervising the work.

This man looked around as Holman rode into the gate opening. The low angle of illumination from the lantern showed him as a lean shape with slightly rounded shoulders and a stubby scurf of black whiskers. Unfriendly eyes looked at Holman questioningly.

The latter said, 'Your name Chess?'

He appeared to consider the question before giving a grudging answer and a shake of the head. 'Anders. Yard boss. What can I do for you?'

'Nothing, really, except maybe give me some information. I ran across one of your stages today. There'd been some trouble; the shotgun messenger was hurt, and the driver—a man named Dempster—was bringing him in for a doctor to look at. I was wondering how he made out.'

For the first time Anders looked interested. So did the other man, who had forgotten his tools to stare at the stranger looming above him on the dun horse. A sharp tilting of the yard bases head let the spray of upward light from the lantern lie more directly across his face as he studied Holman. But his voice, when he answered, was as flat and expressionless as before: 'You mean McCabe. He's dead.'

Though he had more or less expected this, Holman still felt a shock at the finality of it. 'Oh? I'm sorry!'

'No, the doc couldn't do nothing for him. Word come that he'd cashed in, less than an hour ago.'

'I see. Well, he was in pretty bad shape . . . Is your boss around anywhere?'

The heavy shoulders shrugged. Anders answered curtly, 'In the office, I reckon.'

'He keeps late hours.' Holman nodded his thanks and started to back the dun out of the gateway. He could feel the curiosity in the other's stare eating at him like an acid.

'What was your name again?' Anders demanded suddenly.

Though he hadn't mentioned his name, on a perverse impulse he gave it. 'Travis Holman,' he said, and waited for the reaction. He saw the yard boss lift his head with a convulsive suddenness, his eyes widening. The bearded jaw fell open. The workman dropped his wrench. And leaving them to absorb the information, Holman deliberately turned the dun toward the building with the lighted window.

He felt a sour displeasure with himself. It had been an easy and demeaning sort of amusement, and though it came cheap, the price could be high. He thought bleakly, what pleasure can there be in knowing you've made your name something that causes *that* kind of respect? Dismounting stiffly at the bar, he climbed the porch steps, turned the porcelain knob and entered the office of the Rincon Express and Freight Company.

CHAPTER THREE

It had been built and equipped for utility and not for show. The interior walls were unfinished, the flooring of plain pine lumber. A low railing with a swinging gate partitioned off the forward section, where there were benches along the wall for waiting passengers.

Behind the railing were a rolltop desk, a bookkeeper's desk with a high stool in front of it, cabinets and files and a big box safe with a picture of a sailing ship painted on it. A potbellied stove, sitting in a box of cinders, had a fire burning in it; welcome after nightfall at this altitude almost any time of the year. A fine aroma of coffee brewing hit Holman as he entered, starting his salivary glands to aching.

There was a somber atmosphere about the scene that Holman interrupted. Three people were in the room, beyond the railing. A man and a woman sat on opposite sides of a deal work table with china coffee caps in front of them; perched on the high stool in front of the bookkeeper's desk was the stage driver, Burl Dempster. On the opening of the door, all three looked up, and old Dempster quickly lowered the cup from his mouth to exclaim, 'Hey, Frank! Here he is!'

He waved an arm in signal for the newcomer to join them, and as Holman crossed the floor and let himself through the gate, the old man continued: 'I sure couldn't help wondering about you. Couldn't be sure you didn't actually-mean it about riding after those road agents. Alone like that, no telling what you might have run into if you tried it.'

'I tried it,' Holman said. 'I'm still in one piece. I just learned, though, that your friend McCabe ran out of luck.'

'Yeah, it's too bad,' the other agreed, solemnly. 'We all been setting here feeling terrible about it. He was a damned good man—that's what killed him. He just wouldn't pay attention to the boss's orders that he was never to put up a fight . . . This is the boss,' he added then, as though realizing there had been no introductions. 'This is Frank Chess.'

The latter got out of his chair to shake hands. 'I'm pleased to be able to thank you,' he said, 'for stepping in to help this afternoon.' He was a young fellow, who could hardly have been more than a year past thirty. His face was sparely fleshed, his sandy hair thinning, and steel-rimmed glasses gave his mild gray eyes a scholarly look. Holman thought he might have recovered recently from some serious kind of illness. But his jaw was good and his grip was firm enough.

Holman gave his own name, and Chess indicated the young woman seated at the table. 'Miss Allie Baker, my secretary and bookkeeper. I *should* say my gal Friday.'

From the description, Miss Baker could have been one of the efficient female battle-axes who, of late, were beginning to invade business offices and take a place in those traditionally masculine sanctuaries. But she didn't fit that category at all. Either the harp lamp hanging above the table flattered her, or she was quite pretty. Twenty-five at the most, Travis Holman judged, with brown eyes and hair, a stubborn chin, and a scatter of freckles across her nose. In her neat white shirtwaist and gray, ankle length skirt, she made him suddenly aware of the state of his own dirty, horse-sweated clothing and the stubble of his unshaven cheeks. He took off his hat as he returned her grave nod.

Frank Chess was inviting him to pull up a barrel chair from its place against the wall and join them. Miss Baker asked, 'May I pour you some coffee, Mr. Holman?'

'You certainly may.' He got the chair and slacked into it, laying his dusty hat on the floor. To the offer of canned cream and sugar, he shook his head. 'The blacker the better.' As she poured and came back from the stove with it, he noticed with approval the quick grace of her movements, and the trim figure that the severe lines of blouse and skirt weren't able to disguise.

Her hand touched his as he reached to take the steaming china cup from her—and then everyone froze, turning toward Burl Dempster as speech suddenly exploded from the old man: '*Travis Holman!*' Repeating the name that had been so quietly spoken, he stared at the stranger with eyes gone a trifle wild with shock. To Chess he said, his voice raised a note above its normal pitch: 'Hell! You've heard of him, boss! You've heard of him plenty!'

Frank Chess frowned, not understanding; then the delayed reaction came, one that was very familiar to Holman. 'You mean, this is the—the—?'

'The gunman?' Holman finished for him, and at once Allie Baker jerked her hand back as though the touch of his fingers was like a burning brand.

Chess colored slightly. 'That's a harsh name,' he exclaimed.

'When you hear it given to you often enough,' Holman answered, 'you get used to it.' In a stunned silence, he tried the coffee and nodded his approval.

Burl Dempster spoke. He'd got over his surprise, and now he sounded almost angry, as though some sort of joke had been played on him. 'You might have told me!' he muttered. 'Instead of leavin' me to worry about one man goin' after them holdups!' He shook his head. 'But what the hell would Travis Holman be doin' in Rincon!'

'That's enough!' Frank Chess said sternly. 'I'll apologize for him,' he told the stranger. 'I suppose it's only natural to wonder what would bring you to a place as remote as this one. But nobody's prying into your affairs.'

'Well, I haven't been sent to kill anybody,' the other answered coolly. 'If that's the way you imagine I earn my living.'

'I never suggested—'

'But I *was* sent here. I've got a letter for you.'

'For me?' Frowning, the puzzled stage line

operator accepted the envelope Holman took from a pocket of his coat.

While Travis Holman drank from the coffee cup, Chess adjusted his spectacles, looked at his name written on the envelope and slit it open on a thumbnail. In silence broken only by the sound of hammer blows on the underpinning of the big wagon in the yard outside, the others watched him unfold a letter and read.

Slowly the young man's cheeks turned red, as the tide of color spread upward from his throat. His head jerked up, the lenses of his glasses flashing. 'I don't believe this!' he cried hoarsely. 'He wouldn't! He—he has no right!'

'Who, Frank!' Allie Baker demanded in a tone of alarm. 'What is it?'

'Sam Mayberly,' her employer answered, and skimmed the paper across the table to her.

'Mayberly?' echoed Burl Dempster. 'That skinflint?' Suddenly his brow knotted and the old fellows head swiveled to stare at Travis Holman. 'Are we to believe it was *him* that hired you to come here?'

Holman set down his cup. 'That's about the size of it,' he admitted. 'I'd come recommended by someone I did some work for, and he called me into his office. Hearing nothing but bad news from this Rincon Express, he's worried about his investment.'

Allie Baker said quickly, 'He has no investment in this company.'

'Amounts to the same thing,' Holman told her. 'He's made loans, both the bank's money and out of his own private funds. Now he wonders if he'll ever get any of it back. The last thing he wants is having to take over a defunct stage line.'

'The Rincon Express is not dead!' Frank Chess declared angrily.

'It's heading that way,' Holman said, 'if these holdups aren't stopped. Mayberly tells me you're on the verge of losing your insurance. When that goes, the mail franchise goes, too. Meanwhile, the mining company that owns the Princess is threatening to start moving bullion in its own wagons. And you say you're not in serious trouble?'

Chess glared at him. 'You seem to think you know a hell of a lot about my affairs!'

'Only what Mayberly told me. Don't forget, if you go out of business all you leave him is some rolling stock and draft animals that are no use to him at all.'

'And so he sends *you* here without so much as a warning to me! Not a word!'

'The way he put it, it was a matter of time running out. He figured this letter would have to do. When I agreed to tackle the job, he wrote it fast so I could catch the next train west from Gunnison.'

With a bitter expression, Frank Chess took the letter back from the girl and read it again, as though trying to learn more from it than in his first hasty glance. Allie Baker, looking directly at the stranger, asked him, 'And just what is this job, Mister Holman? Are you here to spy on us for Sam Mayberly?'

He answered as civilly as he could. 'No, Miss Baker. Sam Mayberly wants to see an end to these robberies, and to the gang that's doing it—assuming that it is a gang. That's my assignment.'

'A troubleshooter, then . . .'

He nodded. 'You could call it that. I'll work with your local law if I can. But it's got to be understood I do the job my way and without interference.' As he said this, he was aware of the suggestion of arrogance his words might carry, but he was impatient with the hostility he had met in this room. Mayberly, the banker in Gunnison, had failed to prepare him for it, and it roused an answering antagonism which he was too bone weary just now to guard against.

Frank Chess put the letter on the table in front of him. 'I don't doubt,' he said coldly, 'that your services come high. Suppose I can't afford your wages?'

'I've already been paid by your friend Mayberly, a month in advance.'

'I see . . .' The young man started to say something more, then shook his head and closed his mouth and passed the palm of a hand across it. He made an angry gesture. 'So it's all arranged and settled whether I like it or not. Well, I don't like it! Mayberly knows he'll get his precious loans paid—somehow, someday—even if I should fail here. But it's one thing to fail honestly and on your own. What self-respect can I ever have once it's learned he's sent his own man in to take things out of my hands?'

Emotion brought him to his feet, to swing away and stand staring at a black square of window that could have shown him little except his own reflection. Studying the man, Holman had to admit to a certain feeling of sympathy. This Frank Chess had been carrying a load of worry, and his shoulders looked a little bowed with it; from the way his suitcoat hung on him, he had been losing weight. A man with a nagging and continuing concern was apt to be careless about regular meals.

Holman said, 'I can see no reason why anybody, outside the four of us in this room, has to know I was sent. The town can be led to believe you brought me in yourself.'

Slowly the other turned from the window. He said heavily, 'The town may believe it—but *I'll* know the truth!' His chest swelled on a drawn breath; he let his shoulder move and settle. 'All right. Had I any choice, I'd send you back to Mayberly and tell him to keep his nose out of my business. But I'm on the roses! Apparently *I* can't save this stage line; maybe you can. I may hate asking for help, but I'm not in a position to turn it down.'

Holman told him, calmly, 'It takes sense to admit an unpleasant fact. For my part, I don't guarantee I can deliver, but I'll give it a hell of a try.' Picking up his hat, he eased his feet. 'Right now I'm mostly interested in dinner and a bed, if you've got a hotel in this town.'

'Up the street three blocks on the west side,' Chess said. Holman nodded and looked at Burl Dempster.

'I'm sorry again about your friend McCabe,' he said, and got the old driver's curt and vaguely suspicious nod. To the girl he added, 'Thank you for the coffee, Miss Baker.' His gaze held on her face for perhaps a second or two longer than it really had to; but he was male and she was decidedly worth a lingering glance.

Abruptly he turned away and went through the partition gate and across the office to the door. He was certain that their eyes followed him until, without looking back, he let the door close silently behind him.

CHAPTER FOUR

The hammering had ceased with the opening of the door. Outside, adjusting his eyes to the darkness, he saw both the yard boss, Anders, and the workman standing in the gateway to the wagon yard staring over toward the office, with the glow of the lantern on the ground behind them backlighting them and throwing grotesque shadows. Unhurriedly Holman swung down the three plank steps, whipped the reins free of the tie pole. Toeing the stirrup he rose into his saddle and lifted his left hand in a half-mocking salute.

Anders and the other made no move. Travis Holman rode on, feeling their eyes upon his back.

The town itself began a hundred yards or so beyond the freight yard; the twisting wagon road straightened itself out and turned into a street wide enough for one of Frank Chess's big wagons to have turned around in it. Following it, Holman kept his eyes open for three things and spotted them one by one: a crackerbox diner that looked as though it kept late hours; a white frame building with the word 'HOTEL' painted across its upper story; and—keeping the other two for future reference—a livery where he turned in through the gaping doorway and dismounted.

He was examining that hurt foreleg when a Mexican hostler came shuffling up to give the dun a nod of approval. 'Nice horse.'

'If he doesn't go permanently lame on me,' Holman said, and showed him the trouble. The dark face wreathed with concern as the man ran knowing and infinitely gentle hands over the leg, lips forming a soundless whistle.

'Not bad hurt,' he said finally, 'with the right

handling. I fix.'

'You fix,' Holman said, 'and there's a twenty in it for you. I'd hate to lose a good animal.' White teeth flashed in an answering grin, and Travis Holman walked away, relieved to feel that the dun was in good hands and would get proper treatment.

Carrying his saddlebags across his shoulder, he retraced his course to the hotel. In the musty-smelling lobby he signed the register, asked for and got the key to a room on the second floor, front. Handing it to him, the clerk said, 'Staying long, Mister—' and his eyes dropped to check the signature in the book. Holman saw the eyes widen, saw him swallow with the question left unfinished.

'I'll be around awhile,' Holman said briefly, and left him with it while he climbed the creaking steps to the upper hallway.

He gave his room scarcely a glance, knowing from long experience what it would be like—sagging iron bed, water-stained wallpaper, a commode and a couple of stiff chairs. He dropped his saddlebags on one of these, closed the door shutting away the lamp glow from the hall, and stood for a time by the window sizing up the life of the street below.

There was a fair amount of activity for the middle of the week and considering the size of the town. Rincon, he understood, depended chiefly on the crews of the Princess mine and milling works, but there were sheep and cattle outfits in the area, and some lumbering operations to help swell its economic pulse. He looked at the lights of the town's three saloons and listened to the noise that came, muted by distance and the glass of his window. Aware then of the hollow in his belly which the coffee he'd drunk had only partially filled, he turned from the window and had just lighted the wall lamp when a knock at the door announced the desk clerk with towels and a pitcher of water.

The man set them on the commode and left without speaking a word, but with a stare for his guest that held until he backed out of the room and carefully pulled the door to. With a shrug, Travis Holman stripped out of his shirt, hung his gun rig on the bedframe, and proceeded to clean up before going out to dinner.

He had just finished with the towel when there was another knock at the door. He supposed it was the clerk once more, on some business or other, but with a trained caution he reached and lifted the gun from his holster. With the weapon ready he palmed the doorknob, quickly jerked the door open as he stepped to the side.

It was the girl—Allie Baker.

'Well!' he granted. 'Hello!' Surprise nearly made him forget his manners, but he quickly lowered the gun and, stepping back, said, 'Will you come in?'

She was as wide-eyed as the clerk. It

occurred to him that the sight of the gun in his hand, and the naked maleness of deep chest and muscled shoulders, must be a little disconcerting. 'Excuse me,' he said gruffly, and turned away leaving the door open. He laid the gun on the washstand, got a clean shirt out of his saddlebag and shook the wrinkles from it. When he had it on and was working with the buttons, her confidence seemed to return, for she actually came a couple of steps into the room. Holman nodded and smiled reassuringly.

He said, 'You caught me by surprise. Is there something I can do for you, Miss Baker?'

'I'm afraid, now I think about it, that coming here like this wasn't the best idea I ever had,' she admitted. 'But I felt there were some things you really ought to know. I hoped they might help you to understand things a little better.'

'All right.' Holman stuffed in the tails of the shirt. 'Can I offer you a chair?'

He dumped his saddlebags off it and moved it out from the wall. The girl hesitated, then gingerly let herself down with her hands twisted tightly together in her lap. Holman brought the other chair, swung it around and straddled it. On account of the girl he had left the door open, but he wanted to be where he could keep an eye on it.

'I'm listening,' he said.

The girl looked at her hands, then lifted her

eyes to him and set her shoulders as she began. 'This evening, in the office—' She hesitated, then becamc more sure of herself as she continued. It was too bad you and Frank couldn't have got off to a better start, since you're going to be working together. I could see how the two of you seemed to clash from the first word. I thought it might help if I could point out that you hit him in a place that really hurts—his pride!'

Travis Holman inclined his head noncommittally. Given no help, she touched her tongue to her lips and went on. 'Frank *is* a proud man, Mister Holman—and he has a right to be! If you only realized how much he has done with no help from anyone! When he came out to this country, less than three years ago, his doctors gave him six months before the lung fever would finish him. He fooled them all; he fought his way back to health and then, all by himself, he set to work to build this stage and freighting business.

'I don't know if you can appreciate what a victory that was, you being so unlike him in every way. After all, he was a stranger while you're at home in this country. And probably never having to know what it was like, not to own a strong and healthy body—'

Suddenly her face grew pink, as though she'd inadvertently reminded them both of his standing, half dressed, in front of her. The color made her even more attractive, and

Holman began to find himself enjoying sitting here looking at her.

He said soberly, 'I guess I see what you mean . . . How long have you held your job with the stage line, Miss Baker?'

'A little under a year. My father and I came here so he could work in the mine. When he was killed in an accident, Frank made a place for me.'

'I see. Then I imagine you can tell me as much about the situation here as anyone. What about the law for instance?'

'The law,' she repeated, and made a gesture with one of the hands in her lap, an expressive turning of a wrist. 'You mean Pen Shattuck. He's no use! He got his appointment as deputy sheriff here because the sheriff owed somebody a favor. He serves papers and collects taxes from the businessmen, but if there's any danger involved nothing can stir him from behind his desk.'

Holman was impressed by her scorn and her direct way of speaking, very much like a man's. He suggested, 'Then go over his head.'

'The sheriff will never do anything. Not enough votes involved. Even Wade Sorenson has found there's no use putting pressure on him.'

'Sorenson?'

'He manages the Princess mine. Next to us, I suppose he's the most concerned of anyone about these holdups, since it's his company's gold shipments that are getting hit. It could mean his job, I imagine, if the head office in Denver decides to hold him responsible.'

'And I suppose Sorenson blames Frank Chess?'

She nodded and watched for his reaction. Holman rubbed the back of a hand thoughtfully along his jaw. When he suddenly slapped his knees and unhitched himself from the chair he straddled, the girl rose hastily and backed away a step. But Travis Holman merely stood looking at the floor for a moment before lifting his eyes to her.

'It's a complicated setup,' he admitted gruffly, 'but I still don't know what you want from me. You've told me nothing I wouldn't have learned sooner or later.'

'I suppose not. I was just hoping I could keep you from getting a wrong impression.'

'You thought that was worth the risk, picking my room number off the desk register and coming up here, alone . . .'

'Was it a risk, Mister Holman?' she said calmly.

But her expression changed subtly, became guarded, as he walked over to her. Holman came to a stand, codly studying her face. Deliberately then he lifted a hand and placed it on her shoulder. He saw her mouth tighten and even through the cloth of her coat felt the faint shudder that went through her.

'Hell! he grunted as he dropped his hand

away. 'You're scared to death of me! Yet you came anyway—to plead your boss's case. You're in love with the fellow, aren't you?'

He knew at once he had guessed right, even before she said, 'I don't see what that would have to do with it!'

'Could be, a lot,' he answered, and realized it was a pang of jealousy that prompted him. 'Just for openers: Standing here listening to you and looking into those earnest brown eyes, I might not be expected to remember that the owner of a failing stage line could have arranged for the robbing of his own shipments—to make a killing before the string ran out, and leave the insurance company holding the bag.'

The girl had turned white; her breast lifted on a sharply inhaled breath. Voice trembling, she exclaimed, 'Is *that* what you think, you and Sam Mayberly? Is that the real reason you've been sent to spy?'

'I'm not saying what I think. I'm just showing you why I can't afford to take anything that's said to me on trust—not even from you, Miss Baker. In my time I've been lied to by pretty girls often enough!'

Her hand cracked against his cheek with surprising strength. As though aghast at what she had done, she stepped backward; but her eyes blazed. 'I am not a liar Mister Holman!' she exclaimed between set lips. 'And Frank Chess is not a crook. And the less I have to deal with you while you're in Rincon spying, the better I'll like it!' Her mouth trembled as though trying to form more words; then, giving it up, she whirled and went blindly through the open door.

Travis Holman followed her, to stand and watch her move away from him down the streakily lighted corridor toward the stairs. Fingering his stinging cheek, he turned slowly back into the room. By God, she seemed a timid thing at first, but that girl had spirit! And beauty, too, that showed up when anger lifted her from her self-conscious awkwardness. It was a pity things had taken the turn they had and got him off to such a poor start with her.

But then he shrugged his shoulders. He was here on a job; he knew better, surely, than to think such thoughts of any woman. Nevertheless, she was very much in his mind as he buckled on his belt holster and got his coat and hat and, blowing the lamp, went out to find himself some supper.

CHAPTER FIVE

For men to whom Rincon was unfamiliar and perhaps dangerous territory, Sid Flagg and Dillon Cowley rode in boldly enough. Smoke from breakfast fires rose from the town's chimneys, and the wide dirt streets were still streaked blackly with last night's dew. A morning sun, standing just above the eastern ridges, lay warmly on the town and made a dazzle in the windows of buildings to the left of the riders. It was too early for much traffic, but a shifting wind already brought the sulfur stink from the Princess mill.

Cowley, a small-bodied, wiry man, said gruffly, 'I don't like what we're doin'.'

Big, towheaded Flagg told him, 'Stop bitching! There wasn't no choice. You're the only one knows what the fellow looks like, that you turned back yesterday from trailing us.'

'But I tried to tell Luke, I ain't at all sure I'd know him again. I never got a really good look.'

'It's more than anybody else got,' Flagg reminded him. 'So shut up. The trail leads here. The sooner we get Luke the information he wants, the sooner we can leave.'

Dillon Cowley's restless gaze was probing at every doorway, under every porch awning. 'Damn it!' he exclaimed. 'There's a dodger out on me!'

The other scoffed at him. 'Who pays any attention to those things?'

'They do in sheriff's offices!' Cowley subsided, but he nervously fingered the butt of the saddle gun under his knee. A rifle was his weapon, much better suited to his instincts than the six-shooter in his waist belt.

Sid Flagg reached a decision, and, grunting

an order, pulled over to the shaded side of the street and the empty hitchrail fronting a saloon. As he swung down and tied, the smaller man joined him. 'Where do we start?' he demanded sourly.

The big man nodded toward the saloons wide doors. '*I'm* starting with a drink and word with this bartender. You do what you like.'

Cowley shrugged, dropped his leathers across the tooth-marked pole and followed the bigger man up the steps.

* * *

Cash Anders, having dropped in for an early drink, was the only customer. Entry of the two roughly dressed newcomers interrupted the conversation between him and Harv Bergman, the saloon owner, who was working the bar this morning. With an air of impatience, Bergman moved down to the end of the counter as the pair hitched their elbows on the zinc top and called for drinks. He poured, took their money, gave the bar a swipe with his towel and returned to where the yard boss was munching pretzels from a bowl on the bar.

'Just what about this gunfighter?' the saloon man insisted, picking up the thread of their talk. 'This Travis Holman. Does Chess think he's going to save his stage line for him, single-handed?'

Anders shrugged irritably. 'How the hell do

I know what he thinks? Nobody ever tells me anything! I'm supposed to be yard boss, but I never so much as heard till last night when he showed up that the man had been hired.'

'Holman.' Bergman repeated the name thoughtfully, while he swabbed at the bar with the towel. 'Wasn't it him done for Claib Pettigrew, down in Vegas? Yeah, and he was the only one walked away from that dust up with the Sterling boys at Wickenberg . . .' He shook his head. 'You hear so many yarns about a man like that, you don't rightly know how many to believe!' He added, 'Well, if Chess has any notion of saving his line, maybe Travis Holman's his only hope. Len McCabe was a good man, but he sure didn't last long!'

Cash Anders grunted sourly, and finishing off his glass he pushed away from the bar. Back to work, he grunted. 'I got my own job and I do it—regardless of how the boss sees fit to go over my head with his imported fancy gun talent, and not even a mention to me.'

The saloonkeeper picked up the glass. 'I'll be waiting to have a look at this Holman. You know where he's staying?'

'Hotel, I reckon,' Anders said shortly, and he tramped out without appearing to have noticed the pair of riders listening intently at the end of the bar.

They, in turn, gave no sign that what they had been hearing was of any particular interest. They took their drinks in silence, while Bergman pottered about behind the bar and the morning sounds of Rincon came pleasantly through the open door. Finished, they left their glasses on the counter and sauntered outside to stand looking casually up and down the street; a pair of men seemingly with no interest beyond sizing up a strange town.

'That was simple enough!' Dillon Cowley said, as though considerably relieved at the way things had gone. 'We didn't even have to ask a question.'

It seemed, almost, that the two had exchanged tempers. Now it was Sid Flagg who scowled at the run of his thoughts. 'So they're bringing in a cannon like Travis Holman!' he muttered, and swore softly.

Cowley shrugged. 'Let 'em. He'll make as good a target on that box as any other.'

'I'll never believe they'd hire a man like that just to ride shotgun! Yesterday he was right on our trail.'

'And I nearly got him, too, didn't I? Next time—' The little man's head jerked. Quickly he touched Flagg's sleeve and nodded across the street, that was growing warmer as the sun climbed. 'Hell! Why wait for next time?'

Following his stare, Flagg saw the man who had just stepped out of the hotel. Full in the sun, the man stood while he got a cigar burning, and the pair on the saloon porch had a good and uninterrupted look at the compact shape in the brown corduroy coat, and the face darkened by the trimmed mustache. Sid Flagg demanded, 'You think that's him?'

'Well, it's the one I turned back yesterday; I swear to that.'

'You said before you didn't get a good look.'

'I know what I said. But I'm telling you that's the man!'

The cigar was lighted, the match shaken out and tossed into the street. The man they were watching turned and moved along the uneven sidewalk. Cawley started a convulsive move but Flagg checked him. 'Let's see what he's up to.'

They learned in a very few minutes. A half block up the street the wide doors of a livery barn stood open, and the man they thought must be Travis Holman turned in there. 'Come on!' Flagg granted. They quickly mounted their waiting horses and started in that direction, not wanting to crowd their man but determined also not to give him any chance to get away.

As they drew nearer they could see that the low-angled sun, falling directly through the open doors, filled the working area within the barn entrance with a golden glow. Plainly visible there, the man with the cigar and a Mexican hostler were earnestly discussing a dun horse, seeming to examine one of its forelegs. Now the Mexican took the bridle and led the animal back and forth a few steps while the other observed critically.

The target was set up. The question remained how best to make sure of it, and get close enough to do the job without giving warning to their victim. Here on the shadowed east side of the street, nearly opposite the barn entrance, someone was putting up a building of some kind. The floor had been laid and a forest of uprights sketched its sides and partitions; there were piles of clean pine lumber amid the litter of wood chips and trash. The workmen had not yet reported on the job.

Flagg spoke sharply and summoned his companion with a jerk of the head as he turned his mount away from the street. At the rear of the skeleton structure they dismounted and ground tied, while Flagg quickly explained the strategy. Cowley, nodding briefly, snaked his rifle from the saddle loot. Flagg said, 'We may not have more than one chance at him, so make it count!'

Cowley nodded again and, after debating a moment, chose his position. He mounted the flooring of the unfinished building, bootheels thumping hollowly as he hurried through the maze of uprights to the forward corner where some of the rough siding had been nailed up; here he dropped to one knee, beside a gaping hole where a window would go, and propped his rifle barrel. Sid Flagg, meanwhile, had spotted a pile of lumber near the front of the lot, which should give a direct target on the barn entrance.

Sure enough, when he reached his place he found that the golden haze of light flooding the doorway clearly revealed the Mexican, still holding the dun's bridle and gesticulating in conversation. The man with the cigar must have moved farther into the shadows, for at the moment he wasn't in sight. It didn't matter. The instant Holman did emerge into the sunlit street—whether in the saddle or afoot—he would be a dead man. Drawing his belt gun, Flagg felt the satisfying resistance and power of the hammer pull as the web of his thumb clicked it back to full cock . . .

* * *

Travis Holman took a silver dollar from his pocket and spun it into the hand of the Mexican, who caught it expertly. 'Keep talking!' he ordered briskly. 'And walking the horse around. You understand?'

'Si!' The other assured him with a flash of white teeth. And Holman, turning deeper into the shadows, sprinted quickly the length of the barn to the door at the far end. This opened into a corral, where three horses circled uneasily away from him as he headed for the fence. Easing through between the poles, he reached the rear corner of the barn. Checking the open space, he quickly crossed to the adjoining store building, circled its rear and then moved along the far side toward the street. At the forward corner he placed a shoulder against the unpainted boards and drew his gun. Squinting below the brim of his hat into the sun glare above the houses across the way, he had a careful look.

From this angle, the man who crouched behind the lumber pile with his six-gun trained on the stable door was completely exposed to him. Holman studied him, narrow-eyed, and wondered what had become of his companion. The pair had not been out of his mind since he first spotted them watching him from across the street. They had tried to look disinterested but he was not fooled. A man who lived the way Travis Holman did developed a sixth sense for such things. He knew perfectly well there were two men over there, waiting for their victim to show himself—and that the victim was Holman himself.

Carefully he ran his stare over the clutter of building material, and thus caught the faint gleam of a rifle barrel at the window opening as the man who held it shifted position slightly. Holman hesitated no longer. Knowing both would-be ambushers were concentrating on the barn entrance to the exclusion of anything else, he simply moved into the open and started across the wide street at an angle to them.

He was sure the rifleman's range of vision would be constricted by the half-finished wall in front of him. The one behind the lumber pile had only to turn his head, of course, and Holman kept his gun trained that way as a precaution. But he was nearly across now, and with luck he hoped to come in behind the rifleman and disarm him, afterward taking care of the other—perhaps without a shot being fired.

Then, just as he was about to pass from sunlight into the shadow of the building skeleton, the one behind the lumber pile twisted about to call something at his companion and saw Holman. The shock hit him visibly. He yelled as he tried to bring his handgun into action.

A single stride carried Holman out of the sunlight, and a bullet from his gun spoiled the other's shot, causing it to miss. Lunging ahead he gained the corner of the unfinished building, dropped behind the shelter of the raised flooring. Instantly the raw pine boards close by his head brought him a scuffling of boots. Rolling to his knees, Holman saw above him the man with the rifle and fired twice.

The rifle went off in a burst of muzzle flame and a balloon of smoke. A long furrow was peeled out of the clean-smelling pine floor, so close to Holman that he dropped back involuntarily. An instant later came a metallic clatter as the rifle fell, and then the heavier thud of a body.

Rolling again, Holman regained the

building corner and confronted the man with the six-gun, etching on his mind with photographic sharpness the big shape, the broad face, the fringe of untrimmed yellow hair below a battered, grease-stained hat. Both fired without time to aim. Holman felt a streaking blow across his left arm that flung him a step off balance. When he was able to level his gun and squeeze off another bullet, the ambusher had already lunged from sight.

Holman was aware of doors slamming through the town, excited voices yelling. Turning back along his own side of the building, he caught a fleeting glimpse of the fugitive through the skeleton of uprights, fired at it and missed. He started to run. As he rounded the rear of the framework he saw a pair of saddle horses waiting. The yellow-haired man was already on the back of one of them, wheeling furiously away toward the alley and escape.

Travis Holman halted and steadied his weapon for a careful shot that would lift his attacker from the saddle. Even as he did, the silent monitor somewhere in his head that kept track of such things suddenly warned him that he had already spent five bullets, and that the gun was empty.

Swearing, he saw the blond rider flash from sight. But there was still the other horse, which must have belonged to the one with the rifle. He ran forward, catching the reins with his left hand. They slid through his fingers. Only half understanding, he saw the blood that made them slippery. At the same instant the animal caught the hated smell and, whitely rolling one eye, snorted and backed swiftly away. He tried a last time to trap the dangling reins, and then dizziness hit him and he found himself on one knee amid dust and woodchips—the horse escaped, and Holman himself dimly aware, at last, that he was wounded.

CHAPTER SIX

The bullet groove was superficial. Impatiently he wadded his handkerchief and thrust it inside his coat to absorb the blood. Then, before doing anything else, he took time to reload his gun.

By now a small crowd had begun to collect. He had to walk through a group of staring men as he mounted the unfinished building platform for a look at the one he had killed. Holman had never lost a distaste for the sight of death. Face frozen, he studied the figure that lay like a bundle of old clothing, the clean pine boards already soaking up the blood. Leaning, he picked up the rifle; it made him think automatically of that business on the upper meadow yesterday, and of the long gun that had driven him to earth.

Of course, there was no real evidence that this was the same rifle. But that was the way his thoughts ran.

Someone with a nasal, carrying voice said roughly, 'Put it down!'

Slowly, Travis Holman turned. The man who came pushing his way through the group clustered on the platform was red of face, bareheaded, with thinning black hair and the start of a paunch. He wore his striped shirt buttoned at the throat, but no collar. A deputy's badge hung askew on the front of his vest. This, then, would be Pen Shattuck, the sheriff's man in Rincon. He looked as ineffective as Allie Baker and Burl Dempster had said he was. But there was a gun in his hand, and he scowled fiercely as he said, 'You're under arrest!'

Still holding the rifle casually by the balance, Holman looked at the deputy and calmly shook his head. 'I don't think so.'

The other man's head jerked sharply. 'Are you defying the law?'

'You've got no charge against me.'

'I'll decide that!' Shattuck snapped. He had an audience, and from the way he kept looking at them with little darting glances from the corners of his eyes it was clear that he knew it. 'Maybe you deny you're the one who murdered this man?'

'Ask someone who saw it,' Holman suggested coldly. 'The Mexican at the livery, yonder, or maybe one of these men. There were a pair of them, and they had me staked out; I managed to break it up. Whatever that makes it, it wasn't murder!'

The lawman snorted. But now someone pushed forward from the fringe of onlookers, saying curtly, 'You better listen to him, Shattuck. I think he's telling you the truth!'

The deputy's head whipped around. The speaker was a stocky figure, almost bald, with a huge black curl of mustache that all but hid his mouth. From the towel wrapped about his middle Holman thought he might be a bartender or a saloonkeeper. Glowering, Shattuck demanded, 'Did *you* see it, Bergman?'

Bergman shook his head. 'No,' he admitted, 'but I got a couple of notions.' He looked at the stranger with intelligent black eyes. 'You're Travis Holman, ain't you?' And as the latter nodded briefly: 'Anders, from the stage line, was in my place maybe an hour ago, telling about how you had gone to work for his boss. While we was talking, this'—he indicated the body at their feet—'and another fellow come in and ordered drinks. They didn't either one say much, but I got the impression they were doing a helluva lot of listening. And when they'd heard all there was to, they left again.'

Holman looked at the deputy. 'Does that at least satisfy you,' he demanded, 'that there were two of them?'

Shattuck had been staring, his jaw actually fallen open, from the moment the saloon owner mentioned the stranger's name. He recovered now but his face turned beet red. Indignant speech poured out of him, words stumbling over one another as he exclaimed, 'I guess a lot of things are clear, now that we know who you are! We have troubles enough of our own around here without professional gunmen bringing in their personal feuds and turning our town into a shooting gallery!'

'It was no personal feud,' Holman corrected him. 'I never saw either of their faces before, though I do have an idea,' he added, indicating the dead rifleman, 'this may have been the one who used his rifle to turn me back when I was trying to follow sign, after yesterday's stage holdup.'

'You just guessing?' the deputy snapped. 'Or do you have proof?'

'No proof at all. But I might suggest you take a look through the reward posters in your desk, see if you run across his picture.'

'Naturally I was going to do that. I know my job!'

Bergman spoke up. Sarcasm rang in the saloon man's voice. 'That's good news—some of us were beginning to wonder! We ain't seen you doing too much about the ones that are wrecking our stage line. Now, apparently, they've tried to murder the man who was brought in to do the job you can't. But you don't seem inclined to do much about that, either.'

Pen Shattuck rounded on him. 'What the hell do you want me to do?'

'For openers, you could call up a posse. Go after the one who's been getting away from you, all the time we stand here talking.'

It had been the wrong thing to say. Pen Shattuck responded with a weak man's defiance. 'I'm damned if I'll wear out good horseflesh tearing around the country on the say-so of some professional gunfighter! Nobody's showed me yet that it's any of the law's business.'

Travis Holman shook his head. 'Forget it!' he said in disgust. 'I'll get after him myself, as soon as I've done something about this.' He lifted his left arm, and for the first time the others seemed to see that he had been hurt.

The saloonkeeper, Bergman, gave a grunt of alarm. 'That needs tending to! The doc's office is in the next block west. I'll show you.'

'I can find it.' Holman offered Shattuck the dead man's rifle. 'You'll want this,' he said coldly. 'And there's a saddled horse in the alley somewhere.'

The lawman seemed taken aback slightly by the sight of Holman's blood. 'All right!' he said gruffly. 'I'll see to all that.'

Holman walked away and left him with it. As he passed Bergman he gave the saloon man a direct look and a nod in thanks for his testimony. Across the street the Mexican stood watching in the doorway of the barn, an arm shading his eyes; Travis Holman lifted a hand in a brief salute to him.

The doctor's office was not hard to find, a one-story clapboard building with the man's shingle—OMAR TALBERT, M.D.—swinging prominently from an arm projecting above the door. When he entered he found Talbert with his tools laid out and waiting, a neat little man, with bifocals and turkey wattle neck and a white goatee. He laid aside the magazine he had been reading and got unhurriedly to his feet, saying dryly, 'I heard the shootin' so I got ready. I figured the next thing would be somebody bringing me some business!'

Having shed his coat, Holman seated himself and let the bloody shirt sleeve be snipped away. The doctor pursed his lips, clucking a few times as he examined the patient's hurt. 'You're in luck,' he said. 'Difference of an inch or two could have meant a shattered arm. You might have lost it. As it is, nothing much to do but keep it clean and wrap it up.'

'All right,' Holman said with rough impatience. 'Get at it. There's things I should be doing.'

Whatever the old man used on the furrow in his flesh, it burned like liquid fire, but his touch was deft and gentle as he worked with the bandages. 'It's bled all it means to,' he said as he finished. 'Keep using it, don't let it go stiff on you. Come back and let me look at it again in a couple of days, if you're still walking around.'

'You think I might not be?'

Talbert showed him yellow teeth, in a mirthless grin. 'Judging from the rate you're going, I wouldn't be inclined to bet on it.'

Holman paid him and left.

His coat was not too badly damaged, but the shirt was a ruin. On Main Street, he stopped in at a dry goods store and bought a new one, making the change on the spot. Leaving, starting for the livery, he passed the open doorway of the jailhouse and heard Pen Shattuck's voice roughly speak his name. Reluctantly, he turned and stepped across the threshold.

It was a dim and unpleasant room, with high barred windows and a faint tang of urine from the cells at the rear. Shattuck sat behind his desk, a lump of a man with a heavy scowl on his face. He peered at Holman and then, almost with a gesture of defiance, tossed a stiff square of heavy paper on the desk and shoved it forward. 'Thought you might be interested in that,' he granted.

Holman picked it up and looked at a crude but recognizable pen-and-ink drawing of the man he had killed that morning. He glanced over the block of printing below. 'Dillon Cowley,' he read aloud. 'Wanted for robbing the express office at Ouray, two months ago. They want him four hundred dollars' worth.'

'That's a recent poster,' the deputy said. 'Probably part of the last batch, that I hadn't had time to look at yet. I found it right on top of the pile.'

'Does it suggest anything to you?' Holman asked dryly.

Shattuck looked down at his hands, clenched tight on the desk in front of him. He spoke with difficulty. 'If he was an outlaw, and if the two of them tried to kill you, then maybe they *were* part of the bunch that's been working the stages. After you got too close for their liking, they could have been sent here today to nose around and try to find out just who the hell you were.'

It was Travis Holman's turn to take a new look at the deputy. He might not be any bargain as a lawman—touchy, opinionated, and less than eager about doing his job—but seemingly the man was honest enough to admit a mistake. Holman placed the reward dodger on the desk and said, carefully keeping his voice neutral, 'This does make it look—more probable.'

'So I figure.' Shattuck pushed to his feet. 'I should have been on the trail a good part of an hour ago,' he said heavily—probably as close as he would come to an apology. 'Want to ride with me?'

'You'd know the country better than I

would. That would have to be a help.'

Shattuck moved to a rack that held a single saddle gun, took the weapon down and checked the load, saying as he did so, 'I'll get my nag out of the shed.'

'I'll be at the livery,' Holman said, and left.

* * *

The blond rider had certainly lost no time getting clear of town. They picked up the prints where his horse had broken into a gallop from a standing start, followed him as he turned out of the alley into one cross street and then into another, and across someone's unfenced garden plot to break at last into the open, heading for the nearest trees. A thin screen of pine timber cloaked the first rise of sheltering hills enclosing the park where the town stood. Here, Holman pointed out where the fugitive had pulled up, the horse moving around and scuffing the pine litter underfoot, while he waited to find out if there would be a pursuit.

Reassured at not seeing any, he would have ridden on at an easier pace, staying in the edge of the trees as he circled the park. So, at least, Holman explained the sign. Pen Shattuck, apparently uncomfortable in a saddle, merely nodded and accepted the other's reading.

It wasn't too easy following a walking horse through pine needles, but if the blond rider was really unfamiliar with the town and the park, Holman believed he would have left by nearly the same route he had entered it. Sure enough, with Rincon lost from sight behind a dip in the land, the tracks abruptly turned out of the trees and quartered to fall directly into the stage road.

Travis Holman went after them, the deputy following without comment.

Obviously there had not been much travel over this stretch since daylight, and he had little trouble picking out the set of tracks he wanted. But the fugitive must have been afraid of precisely that; after a couple of miles, at a place where the twin ruts swung wide to clear a spur from the shouldering ridge that encroached on it, he had pulled abruptly out of the road. The land lifted sharply. Following, Holman found himself in timber again and presently, through a kind of trough between fallen and slanting slabs of granite, the trail carried him up into broken rock, and there he lost it.

He did not give up easily. With stern determination he began casting about in widening circles, looking for any mark of a shoe or disturbance in the natural lie of the terrain to suggest which way his quarry had ridden. The play was all against him. There was slick rock over which a man afoot, cautiously leading his mount, might have escaped in any of a dozen different directions;

there was even at one place a chute lined with rubble down which he could have clambered, with a shallow rushing stream at the bottom to drown his tracks. Nowhere was there any positive answer.

After a good part of an hour Holman rejoined Pen Shattuck who, having long since abandoned the search, had dismounted and was seated on a fallen log, fanning the flies with his hat while his horse tore at a few traces of grass among the rocks. 'No luck?' the deputy said, and added roughly, 'Wish I could have been of more help, but I ain't any good at this kind of thing. Sorry.'

Holman shrugged and swung down from the saddle. 'I doubt that a Ute Indian would have much luck reading a trail in this country.'

'With as late a start as we've got, I don't think you'd have caught up with him anyway.'

'I wasn't trying to catch up with him,' Holman said. His bandaged arm was aching and he rubbed it as he spoke. 'If he's part of the outfit that's been killing the Chess line, there was a chance his trail might lead me to wherever they're hiding out.'

Shattuck pursed his lips doubtfully. 'I've seen no proof that it's all the work of a single gang. Supposing it is, would they stick to a single hideout? Wouldn't they figure it safer to keep moving around?'

The other was tempted to answer, 'For all the trouble they've had from the law, they hardly needed to have bothered!' But he had decided there was no use needling Pen Shattuck. The man might be basically honest, but that didn't mean he had it in him to make a law officer. Instead Holman pointed out, 'Somewhere they must have a good, solid cache of the gold they've been lifting. That is, unless they've managed somehow to get rid of it piecemeal, and because of the weight alone, that might not have been too easy to do.'

'But the fellow we were chasing wouldn't necessarily have led us to it.'

'Of course not,' Holman agreed shortly. 'Just now he's not leading us anywhere. We might as well admit it and go back.'

The return to Rincon was made in silence, except for once when Pen Shattuck—as though he had been nursing a need to justify himself—said, with an explosive clearing of his throat, 'I guess I can imagine the kind of thing some people may have been telling you about me, Holman. But you have to realize I got no authority. I can't even properly call up a posse; and in these bills, you've seen already that one man by himself can't do much. Since the stage line trouble started, especially with Wade Sorenson breathing down my neck, ain't a week passes but what I write to the county seat asking just what the hell I'm supposed to do. But I get no help at all. It ain't no enviable spot to be settin' on, Holman!'

His voice was heavy with self-pity as he

finished. Holman, feeling sour enough himself with the ache in his bandaged arm, didn't feel too much sympathy. 'Tough,' he agreed shortly, and the matter was allowed to drop.

CHAPTER SEVEN

They parted company in front of the livery, with Shattuck pausing a moment before riding on toward the horse shed in back of the jail. He said gruffly, 'I'll be getting a message off to the telegraph office at Seven Pines about that Dillon Dowley fellow you shot. When it's been confirmed, I can pay over the four hundred reward you got coming on him.'

Holman's expression was cold. 'I don't take bounty money. Give it to Len McCabe's widow if he has one.'

The other regarded him for a moment, then shrugged and rode away. Travis Holman entered the barn and turned the rent horse over to the Mexican. They talked for a moment about the dun which, apparently, was doing well under the care it was getting. Another day or two, he was assured, and the leg would be as good as new. He thanked the man, and walked out upon the street.

To a sound of hoofs and grind of wheels, a horse and rig pulled even with him, and a voice spoke his name: 'Mister Holman . . .' Turning to look at the black top buggy with a bay mare between the shafts, he was surprised to recognize the woman who held the reins. It was the handsome, auburn-haired passenger of yesterday's stagecoach, the one he'd been forced to rescue from hysterics by the only means he knew, and then instructed in the handling of a tourniquet. Mrs. Sorenson, Mrs. Wade Sorenson, of course, wife of the manager of the Princess Mine.

She had either returned from a drive or was about to go for one, judging from the linen duster she wore to protect her clothing. A scarf concealed one side of her face. Travis Holman touched hatbrim to her, and she asked, pleasantly enough, 'Can I give you a lift somewhere?'

'I'm only going to the hotel,' he said. 'It's just a block.'

'Get in.' As he hesitated she added quickly, 'I want to talk to you. It will only take a moment of your time.'

He sensed an urgency in her and complied without any more discussion. She made room for him on the single seat, drawing her skirts aside. Holman settled himself and took, the reins in his own hands and gigged the horse into motion. They rolled through winey sunshine, tinged by fumes of the smelter over at the mine.

The woman had her hands clasped in her lap, the whiteness of their knuckles proof enough of her troubled emotions. She said, without preliminary, 'I'm afraid I made a poor showing yesterday, over that holdup.'

Holman had already judged that she was a woman of considerable pride, and anything that close to an apology must come hard for her. He said, 'I got a little rough with you, I'm afraid. I'm sorry for that.'

'Not your fault I lost my head. But—' He saw her press her hands more tightly together, was aware of the shudder that went through her. 'There's something about the sight of blood! I never have been able to stand it. I don't suppose I ever will.'

'In this country,' Holman reminded her dryly, 'it can be a pretty common sight.'

'I know. That's one of the reasons I hate this country so much, that and the loneliness, and the cold, and the awful bleakness of it!'

They rode in silence during a few slow turns of the wheels.

Holman said, 'You're not from these parts originally, I take it.'

'Good heavens, no! I was born and lived all my life in Philadelphia until five years ago.'

'Philadelphia . . . nice place, I always heard. I've never been anywhere like that far east, myself.'

'I would to God I'd never had to leave!' She added in a tone of weary bitterness: 'But a wife has no option but to follow her husband, wherever he chooses.'

He pointed out, 'Your husband wasn't with you on that stagecoach.'

No answer for a moment; then the words poured from her: 'You know perfectly well I was leaving him. This country is turning Wade Sorenson into a brute, as hard and cruel as the human animals who work under him! I—I just couldn't take it any longer! And the irony is, I almost got away. Except for the holdup and the guard being shot, I'd have made it!

'Well, I missed my chance; I know very well it isn't apt to come again. Not with the spies that will be watching me after this. I don't doubt they're watching us this very minute!'

The buggy had arrived before the hotel's entrance. Travis Holman halted the bay and turned directly to the woman. 'I don't know what you want me to say, Mrs. Sorenson. I do know I can't mix in a family matter.'

'Oh, no. That's never good etiquette, is it?' she said in a note of scorn. 'But *this* is perfectly all right!' And with a movement of one-trembling hand, she drew back the veil from her face and showed the swollen cheek, the eye closed nearly shut, the livid and angry bruise that discolored her flesh.

He flinched despite himself. 'Wade Sorenson did that?'

'Yes. When he found out what I had dared to do!' She added bitterly, as she slipped the scarf back into place, 'Some of the women here think I'm very fortunate, Mister Holman, being married to the manager of the Princess Mine, living in the largest house in town with servants to wait on me. Oh, what I could tell them!'

Without speaking, Holman handed her the reins and stepped down to the wooden sidewalk. He removed his hat. 'I thank you for the lift, Mrs. Sorenson,' he said. 'But as I tried to say before—'

'You said it quite well!' she cut him off. 'I just wanted you to see exactly what you did to me by making me come back!' She slapped the reins against the horse's rump, and the buggy lurched into motion.

Afterward, in his room, Holman was still feeling the shock of that ugly, swollen bruise as he cleaned up and took a look at the injured arm. It throbbed dully, but there had been no more bleeding and he decided it was nothing serious enough to be concerned about. Dressing again, he left the hotel and walked the short distance to the stage line office at the foot of the street.

A buckboard overtook him, spinning up the yellow dust, with one man seated beside the driver and another in the rear, riding backward with his legs dangling and a shotgun across his knees. He seemed to be guarding a metal bound box resting in the bed of the vehicle. The buckboard rolled quickly on, leaving Holman batting at the dust that settled in its wake. When he reached the freight yard, the rig was pulled up before the office door. The driver and the guard, the latter still carrying his shotgun in one hand, had the box and were just starting up the steps with it; it looked heavy.

They gave Holman a suspicious stare, and he prudently stood aside and waited until they had disappeared inside. He mounted the steps then, meeting the pair in the doorway as they came out again. The one with the shotgun seemed to want to stop him, but Holman gave him a pleasant nod and walked inside.

There were three people in the office as he entered: Frank Chess and Allie Baker, and the man who had ridden the front seat of the buckboard. They stood about the deal work table, where the box now sat. It was open. Holman caught the gleam of gold ingots stacked inside, before the man he didn't know dropped the lid into place and worked a multiple set of locks, sealing it.

They were all looking at the newcomer, and Frank Chess made the introductions: 'Sorenson, this is the new man we hired—Travis Holman.'

'I've been hearing about him,' Wade Sorenson commented dryly.

Holman could not have said what he had expected. The manager of the Princess Mine looked about forty, nearly Holman's size but heavier—well groomed, clean-shaven, strongly handsome. The shoulders within his canvas coat held a hint of power. A steely blue stare raked Holman, quickly assessing him.

The resentment Frank Chess evidently still felt was in his voice as he told Holman, 'I've heard nothing all day but talk of the man you killed this morning—and you in town not twenty-four hours yet! Who was he?'

It was hard for Travis Holman to keep his own manner civil. 'A holdup artist named Cowley,' he answered shortly. 'I'm positive he was one of the crew that's been giving you your trouble. We'll discuss it when you aren't busy.'

That seemed to satisfy Chess for the moment. Turning to the girl, he said, 'Allie, do you have that receipt ready?'

Allie had just finished writing it. She handed it to her employer, who signed his name and passed the paper on to Sorenson. As he put it into his wallet, the mine manager said bluntly, 'You realize, Chess, this is against my own better judgment. Supposing this one shipment does get through. What does it prove? Only that we happened to catch them off guard by sending it so soon after the last one. It doesn't get back those that are already lost.'

'I'm aware of that.' Frank Chess looked like a man having trouble holding to his temper. 'We have to take one step at a time.'

'And meanwhile the company's breathing down my neck!' Sorenson indicated the treasure box on the table. 'I'll tell you now: This has to be the last. I don't like to make threats, but my own job's at stake. Lose me one more shipment, Chess, and to satisfy the company I'll have to make other arrangements—even if it means buying wagons and hiring a battalion of fast guns to move the gold out myself!'

'And though it means putting us out of business,' Allie Baker cried, unable to hold it back. Sorenson looked at her and at Chess. With no more answer than a shrug, he turned and walked out. There was the sound of his boots upon the plank steps, and a moment later the buckboard went into motion. They listened to the grind of its wheels and the sound of hoofs fading.

'Will you give me a hand?' Chess asked Travis Holman, breaking a heavy silence. Holman stepped quickly through the gate, and between them they got the chest into the big box safe that filled a corner of the room.

'Won't you want a guard kept tonight?' Holman wanted to know.

The other shook his head. 'There's never been any trouble of that sort. But I always sleep here in the office, anyway, when there's bullion in the safe.'

Holman didn't press the matter. He proceeded to give full details of the shooting of Dillon Cowley, and of his pursuit of the man who had escaped. Allie Baker listened with a rapt expression that seemed to him a mixture of fascination and loathing; but Chess, as though his mind was occupied with weightier matters, scarcely seemed to pay attention. Seeing this, Holman broke the account short, saying abruptly, 'If I'd been able to keep the trail, it might have led to something. But I didn't have that kind of luck.' He picked up the hat he'd laid aside and moved to the door. Pausing there, be indicated the safe. 'I'll be in early tomorrow, and we can make our plans concerning that.'

Frank Chess scowled and nodded. Holman settled for that and left.

He had not eaten since breakfast. On his way to the restaurant to get himself an early supper, he passed Bergman's place and on an afterthought turned back and entered. There were not many customers at this hour. Harv Bergman was just replacing refilled lamps in their wall brackets in preparation for the evening trade. Seeing Holman he came forward, bringing a smell of coal oil with him and wiping his hands on his apron. Holman nodded for the bartender to set up drinks. 'You don't look much the worse for what happened this morning,' Bergman said, observing Holman critically.

The latter flexed his sore arm. 'Shattuck and I took a ride for nothing,' he said. 'Other than that, it hasn't been a bad day.' He nodded his thanks for the drink, adding, 'And I wanted to thank you for stepping in this morning the way you did. I was having a little trouble getting through to your deputy sheriff. Things might have got out of hand, if you hadn't spoken up.'

Shrugging, Bergman touched a knuckle to his luxuriant mustache. 'Pen Shattuck is honest enough, but he's a born fool and the job has made him lazy. You have to build a fire under his tail—and even then you can't be sure anything will come of it. That's why I'm beginning to think it's a damn good thing you're here. Frank Chess had to do something to break out of the box he's in, though frankly I'm a little surprised it would have occurred to him to send for you.'

Holman preferred not to set him straight. A moment later he excused himself to go hunting up the meal he had missed. Turning, he discovered Wade Sorenson standing at the bar with a bottle and a couple of empty glasses beside him. He hadn't been aware that the Princess manager was even in the room. Sorenson gave him a stare and a curt nod, and picking up the bottle and glasses said shortly, 'Come here.' With no more invitation than that he swung away and started for one of the empty tables against the farther wall.

Irritation gave way to curiosity. Travis Holman decided for the moment to swallow the other's crudeness. Exchanging a look with Bergman, he shrugged and followed. A lamp had been lighted in a bracket above the table. Sorenson pulled out a chair and dropped into it nodded at a second chair opposite. 'Sit down and have a drink,' he said gruffly, as he uncorked and poured.

Still standing, Holman shook his head. 'Thanks, but one's my limit on an empty stomach.'

Sorenson lifted a shoulder, set the bottle aside and kept the glass for himself. 'Sit down anyway,' he said. It sounded like an order, but perhaps that was the only way he knew to deal with people. Holman felt a stir of resentment, but he kept it from his face.

'All right,' he said, pulling back the chair. 'But I'm getting hungrier by the minute.'

The other took his time, deliberately, picking up the drink and draining off half of it and setting it down again. He turned the glass between thumb and forefinger as he peered thoughtfully at Holman. Abruptly he spoke. 'I'd say Frank Chess waited till the eleventh hour before bringing you into this thing. Do you honestly think you're going to save his hide for him?'

'I can make a try,' Holman said.

'And if you fail?'

'I've done that before, too.'

Steel blue eyes considered him. 'It takes a better than average man to admit that,' Sorenson said finally. 'Still, from what I've heard, you're not exactly ordinary. I've had reports on that shooting this morning,' he went on. 'From certain parties who witnessed it. What they told me confirms my own impression of you.'

'And?' Holman prodded.

'I'm making you an offer. After Chess goes under, I'll still have gold to move. Only it will become my personal fight and my responsibility. I don't intend to fight it with half measures, as he has done. Come to work for me, and I'll put you in charge of the whole operation, men and wagons and guns. Naturally, I'll pay accordingly.'

Surprised, Holman had to think about this for a minute, probing the various angles. Sorenson said with impatience, 'Well? Do we have a deal?'

'Aren't you getting ahead of yourself?' Travis Holman suggested. 'Chess hasn't gone under yet, so it seems a little early to be picking over the bones of his business.'

He saw the other stiffen, his head jerking up, the very cords of his throat standing out tautly beneath the skin. 'Is that your answer?'

'It will do for now.'

'Then you can go to hell!' Sorenson told him; a strangled bark of sound that burst from him.

Unruffled, Holman got to his feet. 'You may very well be right,' he said with a half-smile. 'Thanks for the drink I didn't want.'

'I won't be making the offer a second time!'

Holman only nodded. He had half turned to leave when Sorenson called him back, his raised voice bringing every eye in the room to them. 'One other thing, Holman! You and Ruby were seen together. That isn't to happen again!'

'Ruby?' Holman echoed the name. 'Do you mean Mrs. Sorenson?' His mouth quirked beneath the trim mustache. 'I didn't know whether to believe her when she told me you had spies watching her.'

'Well, don't forget it!' the man snapped. 'And don't entertain any ideas, where my wife is concerned!'

The handsome features had darkened; the hand had closed upon the whiskey glass. Holman looked at the hand, seeing the strength in it, remembering the livid bruise it had left on Ruby Sorenson's swollen face. Not trusting himself to answer, he merely returned the stare of the glittering blue eyes. Then, deliberately, he turned his back on the man and walked away, the tramp of his heels sounding loud in the stillness of the watching room until the batwings swung closed behind him.

CHAPTER EIGHT

By morning, Travis Holman was relieved to discover much of the soreness had gone out of his arm. He worked with it awhile in the chill of his hotel room, exercising to take the stiffness out of it. Afterward, reasonably satisfied, he finished dressing and went out.

A low ceiling of gray-bellied clouds lay upon the ridges that embraced the town, and he could see his breath. It was a rigorous climate, in this Colorado high country. At the restaurant he had a breakfast of steak and potatoes and bitter black coffee, and then walked through the quiet street toward the freight yard, glad for the windbreaker he was wearing.

Still a hundred yards from his destination, he saw Wade Sorenson leave the stage line office, mount and turn his horse up the street. As the two men passed, Sorenson touched him with a single cold glance and rode on, showing no other sign of recognition. Holman thought: Our little scene last evening still gravels him! He wondered what Sorenson had been doing at the office, this early. Applying more pressure, he supposed.

There was activity in the yard. A stagecoach—the same one that had had to turn back from the aborted start of its run to Seven Pines two days ago—was making up, with a couple of yardmen putting the four-horse team into the traces under Cash Anders's direction. Burl Dempster, waiting, caught sight of Holman and came over to greet him, whip looped around one shoulder. 'Gotta make up for Tuesday,' he said without preliminary. 'Believe me, our schedule's really shot to hell these days!'

'Carrying any passengers?' Holman asked.

'Nope. No bullion either, thank God. So maybe this time I'll get her through. Nothing but the mail sack, and a few odds and ends of fast freight in the rear boot.'

'How soon do you roll?'

'Just as soon as they get them traces hooked.'

Holman said, 'Don't leave till I speak to Chess. I might ride with you.' Not explaining, he moved on to the office where a lamp burned against the murky light of morning.

Entering, he saw that the big safe stood open, and Frank Chess was just in the act of hauling out the treasure box he had stowed inside it last evening. It was a heavy burden for him, and Allie Baker moved quickly to help. Between them they got it placed on the table and then looked at Travis Holman, advancing through the dividing gate. Holman thumbed the hat back from his forehead and, nodding at the box, said, 'I guess we'd better decide how we're going to move this.'

Chess shook his head. 'It's been decided.'

'How do you mean?'

'You must have noticed Wade Sorenson leaving just now.'

'I noticed him,' Holman answered curtly.

'We were discussing the situation. We came to the conclusion it might be worth a try to send this shipment—without a guard, even—in what will look like an empty freight wagon, heading for the railroad to pick up a consignment.' Chess saw the iron in the others look, and he added almost defensively, 'Well, nothing else has worked!'

'I see,' Holman looked at him for a moment. He was conscious of the girl watching. The tick of a tin alarm clock on a shelf was very loud. Travis Holman said then, his tone carrying an edge of harshness, 'Might I ask whose idea this was to begin with. Sorenson's?'

'It was, as a matter of fact. He got it in the night, and so he came down here first thing this morning—'

'To tell you how to run your business!' Holman finished for him. 'Chess, when you signed a receipt for that box, you assumed the risk and also the full authority. What happens to it is no longer any of Wade Sorenson's affair!'

'Now wait a minute!' Chess exclaimed, coloring. 'Don't think I let him twist my arm or anything. I just happened to agree that it was a good idea.'

'Well, I don't!' Holman retorted. 'Do I have to spell it out? Or hasn't it occurred to you that Sorenson could be playing a game of his own? Don't forget, he told you yesterday one more lost shipment would be the last before he cut off all business with your line. It might also interest you to know that last night he did his best to hire me away from you.'

Holman saw this hit the other man. Frank Chess actually blinked behind his glasses. 'Is this the truth?'

The other nodded. 'He was furious when I turned him down. And now comes this maneuver. Think about it a minute. Just suppose he has something to hide. Suppose it's a threat to him, now that an outsider has been brought in, one who won't be bought off. This could be his reaction; a final blow to put you out of business and do away with my job, both at the same time.'

'You're suggesting Sorenson has been involved in stealing shipments from his own mine! It's ridiculous!'

Not at all. Remember, for all the weight he throws around, he's still only a hireling of the company that owns the Princess. And it's certainly no accident the road agents are having the success they do. There's got to be a tie-in or a leak somewhere.'

Allie was sputtering to herself. Now she cried indignantly, 'You're very quick to accuse people, aren't you, Mister Holman!'

She was remembering, of course, how he had hinted two nights ago in his hotel room that Frank Chess himself wasn't wholly in the clear. Holman acknowledged it with a nod. 'You could say I've got a suspicious nature. Still, there's an easy way to check my theory about Sorenson.'

'How?' Chess demanded.

At that moment the door opened and Burl Dempster tramped in, an impatient look on him. 'We're ready to roll,' he told Holman. 'You riding with me, or ain't you?'

'I am,' Holman said. He indicated the box on the table. 'Give me a hand loading this.'

Dempster took one look at the box and backed away from it as though it were coiled to strike. 'Wait, now! We ain't taking *that* thing with us? I was told—'

'That's been changed,' Holman told him, cutting him off.

Allie Baker and the driver both appealed to Frank Chess, with a look. The young man's face darkened; abruptly he swung away, throwing his words angrily across his shoulder: 'Take it along! I don't seem to be giving orders here any more!'

Dempster scowled and muttered something, but he shrugged and stepped forward to lay hold on one of the leather handles. The box was not large, but the solid weight of it gave a hint as to the value of its contents. Together, Holman and the driver took it out and across the freight yard compound to the waiting coach. There, under the curious stares of Cash Anders and the yard crew, Holman stepped up to the hub of the big forward wheel and deposited the treasure box in the boot below the driver's seat. 'One second more,' he told the driver, leaping down again.

‘Don’t hurry on my account,’ Burl Dempster growled. Holman guessed he had been welcoming the thought of a run to Seven Pines without that box full of danger under his boots, and was sorely put out over the change of plans.

Holman had his six-shooter, but his rifle was at the hotel and riding the box he needed a weapon with more reach and power. There was a rack just inside the office door, that contained a twin-tubed shotgun and a carbine. He chose the latter, took it down from the rack and checked the action. Finding the box of shells on a shelf, he dug out a handful and dropped them into a pocket of his windbreaker. His hand was on the knob of the door when his name, spoken roughly by Frank Chess, turned him back.

Chess still looked angry, but he gave Holman a look and a grudging nod. ‘Good luck,’ he said.

‘Thanks.’ Holman looked at Allie Baker but she was bent over her work at the bookkeeper’s desk, and he could see only her profile, broken by the soft line of her hair. He returned the other man’s nod and left with the carbine under his arm.

There had been still another delay. It seemed Cash Anders had decided one of the wheelers, a big bay, showed signs of going lame and had ordered it cut out of the team and replaced. Burl Dempster was striding about, fuming over the way his day was starting. Holman, secretly amused, decided to leave him alone until his temper had a chance to cool. Actually it took only a moment for the substitution to be completed. Still cranky and sullen, Dempster climbed to his place and Holman quickly joined him, propping the carbine against the treasure box.

Dempster laced the ribbons between gnarled fingers. He gave the horses a whoop and a slap with the lines. They leaned into the collars and the battered coach lunged forward, building a momentum as they cleared the gate. They turned into the stage road, and by the time they rumbled over the wooden bridge across the meadow creek, spinning wheels lifting thunder from the planks, Dempster already had his team traveling at a good clip.

'Hope we ain't gonna get weather out of them clouds,' he muttered, slanting a look at the heavy overcast. 'In this country you never can tell. Well, I got me a poncho. Don't look like you brought anything.'

'I've been wet before,' Holman said.

A strong wind was blowing, whipping the clouds along the peaks, combing the timber that clothed the lower hills and the grasses of the Alpine meadow through which the stage trace looped ahead of them. It pummeled the men exposed atop the rocking stage, and made Travis Holman fasten the lashings of his windbreaker.

Burl Dempster was having a little trouble bringing his horses under the fine degree of control he favored. 'It's that damn yaller hoss,' he muttered, indicating the near leader. It was a buckskin, actually, but did look faintly yellow by contrast with the darker hides of the rest. 'I always hate to get stuck with him—got a jaw like iron. Acts like he knows he's different. I always say a matched team's easier to handle. Get along there!' He let the long lash of his whip coil and strike; the popper flicked dust precisely from the buckskin's rump and the animal tossed its head but seemed to settle as the bite of the whip warned it the old man meant business.

Dempster seemed still in a bad mood and Holman, with plenty of his own thoughts to occupy him, didn't press for talk. He was deeply involved in observing details of the country they were traveling. He had been over the route before, coming in on a lame horse two nights ago, but every road looked different when followed from the opposite direction. He said presently, 'I want you to point out, if you will, just where each of the holdups has taken place.'

'I figured you would,' Burl Dempster grunted. 'Keep your eyes open, and you just may get to see the *next* one! And here I was, hoping for once to have a run without no trouble!' He gave the treasure box beneath his feet a kick. 'Gettin' so I hate the very sight of one of these damn things! I guess it's your doing that I got stuck with it this time?'

'My doing,' Holman admitted. 'But whatever you might think, it wasn't just to give you a bad time. I'm checking out a theory.'

A theory about Sorenson?' the old man suggested shrewdly. And getting the other's sharp glance, he added, 'Hell, even *I* got brains enough to figure that! Sorenson ordered the shipment off the coach, you ordered it back on. There had to be a reason.'

'You have any opinions?'

'Meaning, do I think he's the man behind these holdups?' Dempster shrugged. 'I ain't exactly one of his admirers—but if you was to press me, I guess I'd have to say he looks to me like too much talk and not enough brains. That don't have to mean anything, though; I've been fooled before!'

They rode on through the lowering day, the teams running well, now, the miles dropping behind. Presently Dempster stirred himself to announce, 'Three of the holdups, including the one you cut in on, have took place this side of Collier's Station. See them trees ahead? That's one of the places.'

Holman nodded. His restless glance, searching out possible trouble spots, had already marked the point where a dark tongue of pine timber and aspen flowed out of a draw and swept down toward the road, which was hampered here by the steep contours of the terrain. It was an ideal spot for road agents, making it easy for them to get in close for an attack without giving warning. Casually he leaned and brought up the carbine and laid it across his knees, on the alert as the stage brought them in.

The trees swept by and fell behind them; the land opened out again and the moment was past. Holman found a certain tension had come into the muscles across his shoulders, and he frowned and shrugged to ease it, a little angry with himself. He could not afford to grow tight every time he saw a place where trouble might happen. Nevertheless, he left the weapon lying on his lap as he took out a cigar and fired it up. The wind of their passage whipped the smoke away from his lips.

The second place they were looking for was in the bottom of the canyon where he had come upon the stalled coach two days ago. He instantly recognized it: the rushing creek, the draw where he had picked up the sign of the raiders and followed it into the sights of Dillon Cowley's rifle. A few miles farther, the road went up through a gut crowded by slabs of red rock with a few tall pines rising above them. To make the grade the coach had to slow almost to a crawl. Approaching, Holman looked at the old man and caught his curt nod.

'Yup. Number three.'

They crested the climb, were through the narrow pass in a minute or less. As they cleared it, Burl Dempster blew out his cheeks and Holman realized the old fellow had been tense, though he had stubbornly refused to show it.

'That's it for now,' he said, and the relief he felt was evident in his voice. 'No more good places for a bit until we pass Collier's. We might as well relax.'

Holman said nothing. Dempster yelled at the horses and shook them out for the last run to the station and a new team.

CHAPTER NINE

The station, which Holman had seen two days ago while riding in toward Rincon, was modest enough: a one-room cabin with a log barn and a corral. Dempster told him that Gabe Collier, the tender, was a crippled ex-cowhand who managed to live on what Rincon Express could afford to pay for taking care of its stock, eking out an existence with a few crops from the truck garden he had under wire beside the creek that ran behind the station layout. Topping a high point, they had a good view of the buildings: chimney smoke whipping in the wind, horses moving about in the stock pen. Protected by shouldering hills, with tall pine trees swaying beneath the cloud ceiling, it seemed to Holman a pretty good place for an old man to finish out his days. Though in winter it would probably be rugged enough, and helping keep the stage road open would be a chore.

Burl Dempster brought his coach in at top speed, the horses responding as they saw the corral and the end of their part of the run, and hauled it to a standing stop in the hard-packed work area before the barn. As the heavy vehicle rocked on its thorough braces and a ground wind whipped away its dust, Dempster wrapped his reins around the brake handle and yelled a greeting to the peg-legged man in shabby denims who had appeared, bareheaded, in the barn entrance. Cabe Collier only lifted a hand in silent reply.

Leaving the carbine leaning against the seat, Travis Holman swung himself down the side of the coach. He had no warning of any kind. His boots had no more than touched the ground when the voice, behind him in the barn doorway, said flatly, 'Don't turn around, Holman. Put both hands on that wheel and keep them there!'

He could not believe that he had been so easily tricked; yet there had been no hint at all of anything out of normal here. For just a moment a wild, irrational impulse shook him but he battled it down, convinced he would be dead if he risked it. Swallowing a bitter chagrin, he placed both hands on the iron rim of the big forward wheel, and his fingers gripped it hard as he fought for self-control.

Someone was approaching; from the corners of his eyes he saw Gabe Collier stumbling nearer on his peg leg, both arms raised high and an ashen look of fright twisting his face. He was shoved aside and the man who had been holding him captive, with the muzzle of a gun shoved into his back, turned his attention on the man beside the coach. Holman caught the sheen of pale whiskers and unshorn yellow hair beneath the edge of his hat, and recognized the man who had gotten away yesterday morning from the stake out at the unfinished building in Rincon. The companion of the late Dillon Cowley.

He repeated his warning. 'Don't move your hands. Don't do anything at all!' He was so close that Holman could hear him breathing. A hand pawed at Holman's windbreaker, flipped it aside and plucked the gun from his holster. Afterward the hand ran expertly over his clothing, hunting for another weapon. Failing to find it, the blond man gave a grunt of satisfaction and stepped away.

Travis Holman, his thoughts working like an animal in a frantic search for escape, remembered the carbine. Tilting his head he could actually see an inch or two of its barrel, gleaming dully where it leaned against the driver's seat above his head. But with guns trained on him, and wary for the first suspicious move, he knew it was completely beyond his reach.

Now the blond man settled the matter, as he said gruffly, 'All right. Move back from the coach, but move easy. Nobody's taking any chances with you!'

He obeyed, measuring each movement with care. Across the back of the sweating and stomping horses he could see Burl Dempster now, his own hands raised and a look of baffled fury darkening his face. Dempster was being covered by one of a pair of men who had eased from the doorway of Collier's log shack. Two more had emerged from the barn. They were all hard-looking, roughly dressed, heavily armed. They had planned well, moving in and taking over the station before the coach arrived and so gaining command without the need of firing a single shot. Grudgingly, Holman had to respect such skillful management, at the same time he condemned himself for blindly entering the trap.

He turned, dry dirt scraping under boot sole, and got the first clear look at his captor. It was the same one, all right, no doubt of that. He was about Holman's height, a bit thicker through chest and shoulders. His clothing, worn and strictly utilitarian, looked as though he slept in it and probably he did. His jaw shone with the stubble of unshaven whiskers; the lids of his faintly protuberant blue eyes were rimmed with red, as though from disease, and he had a way of blinking nervously.

He looked dangerous enough, yet, facing him, Holman had a feeling he wasn't the chief brains behind this operation.

The man said, 'You're name *is* Holman—ain't it? Travis Holman?'

The prisoner, unwilling to give an inch, lifted a shoulder and said coolly, 'You seem to think you know.'

'Maybe, maybe not,' the other said. 'But it hardly matters, because here's someone who does.'

He looked past Holman, as the latter caught the sound behind him. Quickly the prisoner turned to see the rider who had come into view, walking his roan horse around the side of the barn. There was something definitely familiar about the shape of the man, though at the moment a hatbrim shaded his face. He definitely looked a cut above these others; more carefully dressed, with a certain air of authority they lacked. Spare of frame, almost gaunt, there was yet a hint of strength in the way he sat his saddle.

Like a star performer waiting until the stage is set and ready for his entrance, he came unhurriedly into the center of the scene, into a waiting stillness; and then a lift of his head revealed the face beneath the brim of the man's black hat, and without intention the name came from Holman's lips: 'Luke Griffin!'

A thin slash of a mouth quirked into a

mocking smile; black eyes on either side of a high-bridged nose regarded him. 'You look surprised.'

'I am. I had no idea you were in this section of country. If I had—'

'You'd have known it was me you were dealing with?'

'I think so. I'd certainly have considered it. It's taken brains to manage this campaign against the Chess line—and I just haven't seen that kind of brains around.'

Griffin passed off the compliment, if that was what it was, with the slight turn of a hand. One thing Holman had said appeared to displease him, for, frowning, he hastened to correct it. 'You don't really think I give a damn one way or the other about young Chess? He simply happened to be in thc way.'

'As that shotgun guard was in the way two days ago?' Holman suggested sharply. 'As I'm in the way now?'

'Killing the guard was never part of the idea. I'm not bloodthirsty! He'd be alive now if he hadn't acted the fool. And, friend, *you've* got nothing to worry about at my hands. Not ever. You know that.'

Burl Dempster had been listening to this puzzling exchange, looking back and forth from one speaker to the other with a growing angry suspicion. Now, in spite of the guns trained on him, the old man could hold back no longer. Glowering at Holman, he cried,

'What the hell does he mean, *friend*? What kind of connection is there between you and this bunch of crooks?'

'Not what you're probably thinking,' Holman told him. 'But Luke Griffin and I have met once before, and at the time I had occasion to save his life for him. I guess he feels that puts him under obligations—even if it didn't stop his men from trying to kill me yesterday in town.'

From the suspicion in his stare, the old man didn't look more than half convinced. But Griffin seemed compelled to explain: 'What happened in town was a painful accident,' he assured Holman. 'The boys didn't know any better. They caught wind of your going to work for Chess, and they thought they were doing me a favor. Dillon Cowley paid for his share of the blunder, and Sid Flagg has learned his lesson.' He indicated the blond outlaw, and Flagg scowled but didn't contradict him. 'So it won't happen again.'

'Then what happens now?' Travis Holman demanded.

Griffin raised his narrow shoulders. 'Why, if we've made everything clear,' he said, 'I guess we'll finish what we're here for. Sid!' He gave the blond outlaw a look and a jerk of his head toward the coach.

Flagg nodded and stepped forward, shoving Holman aside. He had gotten rid somewhere of the gun he took from the prisoner. Now he bolstered his own, freeing both hands, and putting a boot to the hub of the front wheel he hoisted himself up. Thrusting aside the carbine, he reached under the seat, caught ahold of the treasure box and hauled it clear, grunting a little at the weight of it. One of the other outlaws came forward to receive it as he handed it down.

With two occupied and the rest watching them, Travis Holman thought he saw a slim chance—foolhardy, perhaps, but pride and chagrin at failure demanded at least a token effort. Flagg's shove had placed him close to Luke Griffin. He turned in a quick pivoting; a groping hand passed over a pair of cased binoculars strapped to the outlaw's saddlehorn, found the stock of a saddle gun. Desperately he fought to drag the weapon from the leather.

He never expected to live to get it clear, but the rifle came free in his hand, and as he swung around he reached for the action, trying hastily to lever a shell into the breech. In the same moment he saw a flicker of movement just above his head and attempted to duck away from it, but not in time. He knew exactly what was happening to him seconds before the barrel of Luke Griffin's six-shooter completed its brief arc and the hard metal struck. Cushioned by the material of his hat, it still seemed to him that it sank deep into his skull.

There was blinding pain, and the brightness of suns exploding in his face. Then the day turned to darkness and he fell into it, his limbs bound in lead.

His head felt mushy as a melon and twice as big. When he tried to move, waves of pain and nausea went through him. He lay carefully motionless for long moments while he waited for them to pass, and tried to decide whether a muffled drumming roar he thought he could hear was actual sound, or something conjured up by his addled brain.

Presently, with greater caution, he of his eyes open and found he'd been placed—fully clothed, even to his boots—atop the blankets on someone's pole bunk. His guess that he must be in Gabe Collier's shack was confirmed when the clomp of the cripple's peg leg approached across the puncheon flooring. Collier moved into sight, to stand scowling down at him.

The station tender was probably a younger man than Burl Dempster, but the loss of his leg had aged him and dried him up into a vinegary husk of a man. It had given his bearded face a perpetual sourness, that showed now as he looked at Holman and said, 'So you come out of it! I was beginning to wonder if you would.'

Holman ran his tongue around inside his mouth. It seemed to be covered with fur. 'How long have I been lying here?'

'Couple of hours.'

He swore, a trifle weakly, and willed himself

to sit up. The effort set his head spinning but he made it, afterward clinging to the frame of the bunk while the throbbing in his skull reached new peaks and then gradually settled. The cripple watched, shaking his head with disapproval. He stumped away, returning a moment later with something in a tin cup which he offered his guest.

'This might help.'

It was raw whiskey. Holman drank it, shuddering a trifle at its potency, but almost at once he felt the boost it gave him. He still did not feel ready to try gaining his feet. Handing back the empty cup, he asked the next question that came urgently to his mind as it began to clear: 'Where's Dempster? Is he all right?'

'They never hurt him any. Soon as they was gone and we'd got you inside, he went on to finish his run—even without the bullion, there's still the mail sack had to get through.'

'They left that?'

'So far they ain't ever touched it. Burl figured he wouldn't have any more trouble between here and Seven Pines—for all the good that does him!'

Holman felt his skull, gingerly. The blow of Griffin's gun-barrel, cushioned by his hat, had failed to break the skin, but there was a bad and painful lump in the thick mane at the back of his head. A more direct blow would probably have crushed the skull; as it was he hoped he hadn't taken a concussion.

The cripple's voice seemed to come as from a distance. 'They sure played me for a damn fool! I swear I never thought a thing of it when that squint-eyed blond fellow—the one I heard 'em call Flagg—come riding in a few minutes before the stage was due. I waltzed right up to him, just like I was a stray pup glad to see company, and stood there while the bastard put a gun on me! Then he signaled in the rest, and they put their hosses in the barn so as not to give away that anything was afoot. Then they simply staked the place out to wait for you to come barreling into their hands. I ain't too proud.'

Holman shrugged. 'I didn't do any better. They should never have got my gun that easy.'

'They left it for you,' the cripple said; he brought the weapon from a table and handed it to its owner. Holman checked the action and the loads and returned the weapon to its holster, which was still about his waist. Collier continued, 'And Luke Griffin—if that's who it was in charge—he give me a message I was to deliver whenever you come to.'

Holman gave him a look. 'Oh!'

'He said, "Tell him I figure this makes it dead even." Them was his words. Maybe you can figure what they mean.'

'It isn't too hard,' the other said bleakly. 'Griffin could have killed me, as easy as not. By sparing my life this time, he probably considers he's squared what he owed me for the mistake I made once by saving his.'

Collier gave a grunt. 'Wasn't that generous as hell!'

'By his way of thinking. Now things are balanced between us. Griffin wants me to know that next time there'll be no holds barred.'

Holman set his teeth and pushed himself up off the bunk. He thought for a second he would not be able to make it, but he toughed out a new wave of dizziness and pain that bit him. He ignored the disapproving shake of Collier's head, and asked, 'Would you have a horse and saddle I can borrow?'

'Maybe,' the old man said. 'But what the hell for?'

'What would you imagine? I've got to pick up a trail!'

'I bet you don't,' the other retorted, and cocked a look toward the roof above their heads. 'Do you mean to tell me, you can't hear that?'

Holman became aware again of the drumming noise that he'd noticed on waking. It had kept on without interruption, behind their talk, and he suddenly recognized it for what it was. There was a window near the bunk and he turned and walked over there on unsteady legs to look out at the heavy downpour of rain spilling from the black sky. He swore, and behind him heard the cripple say, 'Any sign that them outlaws might have left will of been plumb washed out by this time. *Nobody's* going to pick it up!'

Travis Holman considered the dreary, half-drowned world beyond the window, knowing the old man spoke the truth. But as he turned back into the room, he said, 'I'll still need the horse. I'm doing no good here. I have to get back to Rincon.'

The other stared at him. 'You really must be sick in the head! You're in no shape to ride. A man don't take a gun barrel across his skull, without he feels it awhile. Why don't you wait till tomorrow? The stage will be coming back through and you can go in that way.'

'I'm not being paid to sit around here doing nothing,' Holman told him gruffly. He took a step and went down upon his face.

CHAPTER TEN

He awoke again, to a bleak morning and an aching head. By moving carefully and deliberately, he found he could manage despite an occasional attack of dizziness. A cup or two of black coffee laced with Collier's whiskey helped considerably. 'You *look* better,' the crippled station tender commented. 'How do you feel?'

'I'm on my feet, anyway,' Holman said. He

walked to the window for a look at the day. It had rained through a good portion of the night, but now the cloud ceiling was breaking up and a weak sunlight lay upon the timbered ridges.

Travis Holman dressed and strapped on his gun, while Collier watched with scowling disapproval. It was when he reached for his hat and coat that Gabe Collier demanded, 'Where the hell do you think you're going? That stage ain't due back through until noon.'

'You don't think I'm going to sit around playing solitaire, while I wait?' Holman retorted. 'If I can have the borrow of that horse, I mean to have a look in the direction that bunch of Griffin's took leaving here.'

'I told you yesterday it would be a damn fool waste of time and strength,' the cripple said gruffly, lurching up off the bench where he had been sitting. 'But if it's what you want I'll go throw on a saddle for you. I doubt you'd be in shape to lift it.'

Holman had no real hope of accomplishing anything after that flooding rain. Still, his frustrations demanded to be worked out in action, and, at any rate, it would be part of his job to search out any possible trail. But Collier had been perfectly right about it. Though he spent an hour casting about, limiting out and following each draw or gully that the outlaws might have used when they left the flat and mounted into the hills, there was nothing to be seen. The beating of the storm had washed away every sign.

Before he turned back the sun was high, the clouds largely dispersed, the ground steaming. Collier, at work in his root garden, shaded his eyes with an arm until he identified the horseman, then set his hoe aside and came pegging to take the horse as Holman stiffly dismounted. Seeing the look on the other's face, he needed to ask no questions.

The stage rolled in at noon, on schedule, with a couple of passengers inside: a drummer, and a businessman returning to Rincon. They got out and hurried into the station for dinner, passing Travis Holman, who waited in the doorway while Burl Dempster climbed down from the boot. Seeing him there, the old driver halted perceptibly for a moment with one hand on a spoke of the big coach wheel. He came on then, but Holman could see the unfriendly scowl that darkened his face.

'No more trouble?' Holman asked, and got the briefest of looks and a bare shake of the head. Dempster tramped past him into the building, saying nothing at all; Holman's mouth settled in grim lines.

He managed to hold his patience while the meal stop was completed and the teams changed, and the passengers returned to their places: Within twenty minutes of its arrival the coach pulled out again, on the last leg of the run to Rincon. Holman, seated on the swaying high seat, waited to give Burl Dempster a chance to speak. But the old driver seemed bent on ignoring him, giving all his attention to the horses and particularly to the 'yaller' buckskin with which he seemed to share a long-standing feud.

Finally Holman had had enough. 'All right!' he said tightly. 'You've got a bone in your craw and you better spit it out before it chokes you. Or have you quit speaking to me for good?'

The old man shot him a hard look. 'I got nothing to say that you'd enjoy hearing,' he answered, and yelled at the teams as the coach maneuvered a long and twisting descent through rocks and crowding pine. When the vehicle had leveled out again, along a sage-dotted bench, he added, 'Any talking *you* might feel like, it's no sense wasting on me. You better be figuring how you're gonna tell Frank Chess his stage line has gone bust—thanks to you!'

Holman kept a grip on his temper. 'Perhaps you're thinking I don't blame myself for what happened yesterday. I know I made a stupid mistake, letting myself be tricked the way I did.'

'What makes you think you know what I'm thinking?' the old man retorted, in a tone that brought him Holman's stare.

'Do you believe I'm tied in somehow with Luke Griffin?'

'I've had twenty-four hours to chew the

thing over, and I can't see it any other way. Hell!' He spat across the turning wheel. 'You've admitted he's a friend of yours.'

'I've only admitted knowing him.'

'I wouldn't even want to admit *that*. I think I'd hate to live in your world, Holman!'

That stopped Travis Holman. He could find no ready answer, during a long silence while the team kept up its steady, slogging gait. Even the troublesome buckskin wheeler had settled into the rhythm now. The coach rocked and swayed over the uneven wheel ruts, and sunlight and cloud shadow flowed across a broken land.

Finally, drawing a breath, Holman said, 'You've been around awhile. You know by now a man don't always choose his path. He takes a first step, and that leads to a second, and by then it's not always easy to turn back. That's how it was with me.

'I'm not trying to justify myself,' he went on bluntly. 'About Luke Griffin: A couple of enemies laid for him one night, in an alley leading into the plaza at Santa Fe. I happened along, saw the setup and managed to break it up. I'd never met the man before and I've never laid eyes on him since that night, never again until yesterday. Still, an outlaw like Griffin can have peculiar ideas of honor. Apparently he thought he owed me—and after sparing my life at Collier's, he thinks now the debt is paid.

‘Whether you believe me or not, that’s the whole story.’

He looked at his companion, saw Burl Dempster scowling at the dusty backs of the horses. For a moment there was silence except for the rhythm of hoofs and wheels and the slam of timbers as the coach jarred across a chuckhole. When the old man spoke, his tone was flat and unyielding.

‘What I might believe cuts no ice. And it sure don’t get back that strongbox! *Nothing’s* gonna do that. And we both know what it means to this Goddam jinxed stage line.

It was his only answer. Travis Holman gave up the effort of talking. They lapsed into a brooding, unspeaking silence.

* * *

When there were passengers for Rincon, the coach took them on into town and unloaded in front of the hotel. It made an abrupt turn at the corner, stopping long enough to deliver the mail pouch to the postmaster, who came out of his general store, in apron and alpaca sleeve protectors, to take it as Burl Dempster tossed it down from the boot. Afterward, with an empty coach, Dempster rolled back down the long street and in through the gate at the stage yard.

Holman could have dropped off at the hotel, but he would not sidestep what lay before him. He stayed on the coach. When it rocked violently to a halt, as the old driver kicked on the brake with savage temper, he took his carbine and swung down the high wheel. He turned to face Cash Anders.

The yard boss had come from the blacksmith shed and was approaching with a look of undisguised interest on his swarthy face. 'Well?' he demanded loudly; and getting no answer looked to Burl Dempster as the latter came around the rear of the coach. 'How did it go this time?'

The old driver gave him only the shortest of looks, but his expression must have told Anders everything. The yard boss switched his stare again to Holman, and his muddy eyes lighted and his beard-stubbled lips pulled back to show his teeth. 'By God,' he exclaimed. 'It really happened, didn't it? You lost the shipment! You that was gonna show us all how much smarter you was!'

'Just shut up!' Burl Dempster muttered.

Anders lifted his stare toward the office door, as it opened and Frank Chess appeared. 'You hear?' he called loudly. 'This imported gunhawk you brought in over my head has done no better than—' But at that moment he caught the edge of Travis Holman's glance, and something seemed to stop the words on his tongue. The speech trailed off, and then Holman pushed past him toward the office steps.

He saw consternation in the face of the young man awaiting him there. Cheeks gone white, Chess moved aside to let him enter. Without speaking, Holman put the carbine into the wall rack. He looked toward the stove, where the coffee pot sat in its usual place, and said gruffly, 'That smells good.'

Chess looked at him closely, as though he could see in the other's face some trace of physical pain. He said quickly, 'Sit down. I'll pour you some.' Holman thanked him with a nod and, going to the work table, dropped into a chair and put his hat beside him. A sour lethargy lay upon him, and his head throbbed wickedly. He passed a hand carefully across his scalp, scowling as it touched the tender swelling Luke Griffin's gun barrel had put there.

Then Frank Chess placed a steaming cup in front of him. As he drank, Burl Dempster entered the office, closed the door and remained standing by it, watching. To Chess, who had taken the chair across from him, he said without preliminary, 'They hit us at Collier's. They had taken the man prisoner, and they made him wave us in. We were surrounded before we had a hint that anything was wrong.'

Chris had his hands clasped tightly. He swallowed once before he said, 'And—the box?'

'They got it.'

He waited, expecting almost any sort of bitter tongue-lashing. Instead, a quiet mood of resignation—or perhaps of despair—appeared to have settled over Frank Chess. His head bent, he drew a ragged breath and opened his hands and pressed them hard, palms flat, upon the table.

A savage feeling of guilt made Holman say, bluntly, 'There's no one to blame but myself. I had a theory and I insisted on testing it—over your objections. So, it's wholly my fault.'

'What does it matter whose fault it is?' the other man said, his tone almost expressionless. 'You did your best, as you saw it.'

Holman drained off the contents of his cup. 'There's more.'

That brought an explosive snort from Burl Dempster. 'I was wondering,' he stated harshly, 'if you were gonna tell the rest of it!'

Frank Chess lifted his head sharply, peered through steel-rimmed glasses. 'What do you mean?'

Holman proceeded to relate exactly what took place at Collier's Station. He held nothing back. He told about Luke Griffin and, once again, explained what lay behind the outlaw's notion that he owed Travis Holman for the saving of his life. He ended: 'There you have the whole story. I don't know what you'll make of it. Perhaps you peg me for a liar and a turncoat—and you wouldn't be the first!'

He heard Burl Dempster, over at the door,

mutter something and shift his boots. Chess was frowning, staring intently at Holman. He said slowly, 'Luke Griffin . . . It's a name I hadn't heard.'

'This is new country for him. Maybe things got too hot for him; down in his usual territory. Or, he had things picked too clean.'

'But, hold on!' the other exclaimed, animated now by a sudden thought. 'Perhaps now there's a chance of getting some real help from the law. If we let the federal marshal know who we're up against . . .'

Travis Holman shook his head. 'Federal law isn't interested in Griffin. He's no fool. You've noticed, in all this time, he has never once touched a mail sack—and he won't. He knows better than to cross that line.'

'I see.' Frank Chess lost his brief animation. 'I see what you mean.' He pushed heavily to his feet, walked over to the stove where he picked up the coffee pot as though about to pour himself a cup, then put it down and stood staring at nothing, overwhelmed by his own dark thoughts.

'I'm afraid it doesn't help any, simply knowing that Griffin is the man we're dealing with,' Holman went on. 'Since we still don't know how he manages his steals: where he hides out, and how he always seems to know which shipments to hit. I really thought for a while Wade Sorenson might be guilty, but we proved there was no way for him to know that box of bullion was going out on the stage, instead of in that wagon as he wanted. So the only positive notion I could come up with turned out wrong. We're right back where we started.'

'We ain't even there!' Burl Dempster retorted from the doorway. 'What *I* see is that this outfit has just played out its string. Sorenson wasn't just yappin' when he said he was through fooling with us. That was the last shipment we're ever going to have the chance to lose for him—and without him and his Princess Mine, we all know how long we got any hope of staying in business!'

Chess turned from the stove, moving slowly like a man with a tremendous weight settled on his shoulders. 'Perhaps it isn't that bad,' he said, but he spoke without conviction. 'This has been a blow, but let's not throw in the sponge yet.' He looked at Holman. 'You must be exhausted. Perhaps you should have Talbert look at that dent in your skull, and then get yourself some rest.'

Rising, Holman picked up his hat. 'The skull will do,' he said gruffly. 'But I'll go along with the rest of the suggestion. You want me for anything, I'll be at the hotel. Otherwise, I'll see you in the morning.

He drew on the hat, carefully, and walked out of the freight line office. He left a moody silence behind him.

CHAPTER ELEVEN

By nature Holman was a light sleeper. This time—drugged by fatigue and the lingering effects of the blow on his skull—his instincts failed him. On some unconscious level he must have been aware of the tramp of heavy boots through the hallway, the low mutter of voices, the turning of the knob. The door, flung open, crashed against the wall. He was still trying o rouse himself to wakefulness when a hand fell upon his shoulder and a voice said harshly, 'All right, you! On your feet—you're wanted!'

He started violently then subsided as he brought into focus the pair standing beside his bed, and the glint of a revolver in the hand of one of them. He blinked to clear his head. He could not have slept long. There was still strong daylight at the window. Looking past the intruders at the open door, he realized that—for once—he had forgotten to lock it before throwing himself on the bed. He could not remember ever having made that mistake before.

He was fully dressed except for his boots. Shell belt, holster and gun hung over the back of a chair next to the bed One of the men, seeing his eyes move in that direction, kicked the chair aside. 'You won't be needing that!'

They had him hopelessly disadvantaged and

they knew it. It must give real satisfaction to would-be tough cases like this pair, seeing a man of Travis Holman's reputation unarmed and subject to their whim. When he levered himself to a sitting position on the edge of the bed, the one who held the gun scooped up his boots and tossed them at him, saying, 'Put 'em on!' He took time first to give his captors a deliberate appraisal. Neither one looked familiar, but from their rough clothing, stag pants and miner's boots he was beginning to get a notion of what he was dealing with. Not arguing, he pulled on his boots and stood.

The revolver motioned him toward the door. Holman turned that way, and they fell in close behind him.

Below stairs, the lobby was unoccupied. Holman let himself be herded through it onto the veranda. As they emerged, someone stepped out through the batwings of Bergman's saloon across the way. It was Wade Sorenson. He stood a moment holding the doors apart. Then, as the trio from the hotel tramped down the steps, he let the panels swing to behind him and came forward, circling past a vacant hitching rack and moving into the street. He met Travis Holman in the center of it.

The street was slick with mud. Puddles stood in it from yesterday's rain, their surfaces ruffled by a crisp breeze that had just sprung up to pluck at the skirts of the mine manager's corduroy jacket, at Holman's bare head. Holman was aware that the man with the gun had put it away as they came into the open, but he would have it handy.

Face expressionless, he met Sorenson's stare.

He thought he had never seen a man so angry. His eyes blazed with it. His mouth, tight-clamped, worked as speech tried to form and come pouring out of him. He raked Travis Holman from head to foot and back again with his furious glare, and then the words came in a voice that carried loudly along the empty street: 'All right, by God! Let's hear you say it to my face, if you've got the nerve. Tell *me* that I've been stealing from the company I work for!'

Travis Holman drew a breath, let it out. 'I suppose it was bound to get back to you. I made a mistake, and I can't blame you for not liking it. But I was hired to do a job and I had to look at every angle. Surely you can see—'

He didn't get to finish. A rocklike fist came over, smashing for his face. Holman saw it coming but had no chance to block or retreat. He pulled his head to one side and the blow took him high on one cheekbone, filling his head with crushing pain and driving him back. He collided with one of the pair who had fetched him from the hotel, and went down in the mud.

Through the ringing in his head he was

aware of Sorenson's raging voice. 'This time you've got no gun to hide behind. Now on your feet!' Holman tried to oblige. He got both hands against the ground and prepared to lever himself up, but he failed to move quickly enough. 'Pick him up,' Sorenson ordered. 'Hold him if you have to!'

Hands laid hold of him and he was hauled unceremoniously off the ground, with Sorenson's henchmen each gripping him by an arm. There was a confused glimpse of sky, of colorless frame buildings that lined the street, and of the faces of the people who had appeared from somewhere to watch from a safe distance as he took his punishment. Then, before he could set himself, a shadow fell across him and Wade Sorenson's sour breath gusted as the man swung with both fists. One struck him on the forehead, the other smashed against his chest and drove the wind out of him. His knees sagged.

Sorenson bellowed at his men: 'Damn it, I said hold him!'

Holman was straightened with a savage jerk, and one of his captors dealt him a vicious blow against a kidney that fairly lifted him onto his toes. 'That's better!' Wade Sorenson grunted, and struck him in the face. Instantly blood filled his mouth from a cut cheek.

A new voice cried harshly, 'That's just a plenty of that, damn it!' To Holman it sounded like the saloonkeeper, Bergman. Lifting his head, he saw the man among the small crowd that had collected on the farther walk. Bergman had something in his hands that gleamed with sunlight striking metal—the polished metal of a shotgun's tube!' Sorenson he warned. 'There's a couple too many out there. You tell your men to back away and stay out of it.'

The mine manager rounded on him. 'Mind your own business, Bergman!'

'Be glad to,' the other retorted. 'But this shotgun has got a nervous trigger—and if it was to go off, it would just about scatter your kneecap.'

There was a long moment; then, in poor grace, Sorenson growled an order at his men. At once, Travis Holman was released, so suddenly that he almost fell again but managed to stagger and catch his footing. Satisfied, Bergman lowered the shotgun. Holman swallowed, gagged on the taste of his own blood and spat.

That was all the time Sorenson allowed him. Suddenly the man was lunging at him, boots splashing muddy water. Trying to evade the rush, Holman took a blow on the side of the head and found himself down again. But this time he was not so badly hurt that he failed to see the danger as Sorenson lifted a boot to stop his face into the mud. With a muscle-wrenching effort he managed to avoid it. His hand caught the descending boot and jerked, and Sorenson, off balance, yelled as he went spilling down into the street.

Fury exploded in Holman then, cutting through pain and fatigue, as he came rolling to hands and knees. When Sorenson floundered up out of the mud, Holman was already on his feet and waiting. He plunged forward and one fist found Sorenson's jaw while the other took him solidly in the ribs.

Clearly the man was caught by surprise. After a single backward step he set his heels and swung a little wildly. Momentum carried Holman inside his reach. Blocking the fist, he countered with a hard chop that sent a pleasant jar of pain running up his arm. Sorenson was hit solidly on the side of the skull, and this time he was the one to be flung aside, spinning half around. A boot slipped and he dropped briefly to one knee.

Holman spat another spray of blood and closed again as Sorenson scrambled up to meet him. He batted aside the other's defense, his fists working like pistons. The man's nose went in a smear of blood and smashed cartilage. A blow managed to graze Holman's cheek, but it lacked steam; suddenly, in the sweating and bloody face in front of him he saw only pain mingled with the beginning of fear.

Sorenson was stumbling backward now, no longer even pretending to fight. Whimpering, he threw both arms in front of his face but

Holman continued to deal him punishment. Dimly he seemed to be aware of voices yelling in the background; all he could see was the face in front of him and he worked on it with a terrible concentration. A hitching pole halted Wade Sorenson's retreat. Pinned against it, he stood and absorbed the weight of Holman's fists until his knees gave way, suddenly, and every joint in his body went loose and he slid down to land on his face. And Travis Holman, coming out of the fog of rage with a convulsive shudder, stood and looked blankly down at him.

He had never really got over the effect of the blow he had taken from Luke Griffin's gunbarrel, and Sorenson's fists had punished him badly. Shaking, Holman leaned a hand on the tooth-marked hitchpole. Seeing the damage he had done to the man at his feet, he felt a sudden revulsion. He lifted his head to meet the stares of a silent crowd of onlookers.

Harv Bergman, still holding the shotgun, caught his eye and nodded as though in approval. That reminded him of the pair who had brought him out of the hotel and held him for Sorenson until warned off by the saloonkeeper's weapon. He looked for them. They stood to one side, scowling blackly, but he thought he saw respect in them, and even a hint of fear as they looked at what he had done to their chief. He said roughly, 'I don't think he's too badly hurt. Just the same I suggest you get him up from there and take him to the doctor.'

'No!'

The exclamation brought his head around sharply. He hadn't noticed the buggy. It must have rolled to a stop at some moment while the fight was going on. To his dismay he looked into the face of Ruby Sorenson and saw it drained of color.

'No,' she said again. One of the pair of henchmen, who had begun a step forward, drew back his boot and looked at Holman uncertainly. And while the crowd watched, she got down from the buggy. Unmindful of the mud and slop of the street, she knelt by Wade Sorenson and touched the bloody, swollen face.

She raised her head then to Holman. 'Will you help me?'

'Of course.'

He lifted her to her feet, then leaned and caught the hurt man under one arm. Sorenson was a compact and solid weight, difficult to handle. He groaned and opened his eyes but seemed unable to do anything to help himself. Holman, shaky enough himself, had to lean his weight against the hitchpole for a moment while he shifted his hold and passed the man's arm across his own shoulders. Then, with Ruby on her husband's other side and doing what she could to help, Travis Holman half dragged, half carried him to the waiting buggy while the crowd watched in curious silence.

It was no easy task to hoist the limp weight onto the buggy's seat, but somehow Holman managed. As Ruby returned to her place and took the reins, Holman squeezed in beside Sorenson and helped to steady him there. The woman spoke to the buggy horse and, sawing the reins, made a cramped turnabout in the middle of the street. She got the buggy straightened out and sent it rolling slowly along the puddled, rutted thoroughfare. Sorenson's head, sunk onto his chest, wobbled helplessly to the motion.

Looking across him at the woman, Holman tried to find something to say, but she seemed grimly intent on her driving. They rolled through the street, past the jail and the livery barn and the unfinished frame of the building where he had been ambushed and had shot Dillon Cowley. At the corner where he had thought she would turn down toward the doctor's office, Ruby Sorenson kept going ahead without slacking speed. Travis Holman started to say, 'Just a minute! You've passed—' But a glance at her face told him she knew just what she was doing. Puzzled, he settled back to find out where she was taking them.

He had already noticed the big frame house that stood alone at the extreme north edge of town, amid trees in a green lawn, with a barn and other buildings behind it. He could scarcely have missed it: an imposing structure in wooden Gothic style, with dormer windows breaking the line of its steep roof, a round turret like the keep of a medieval castle, and deep verandas on all four sides; the eaves dripped with scroll saw ornaments. It was truly an elegant dwelling place, Travis Holman thought, except for the stink of smelter fumes that hung everywhere in the park when the wind died and failed to carry it away.

Someone was chopping kindling. As Ruby Sorenson turned into a graveled drive and halted near the side entrance, a yardman looked up from his work at the chopping block. She called, and he left his ax sticking in the wood and came hurrying. He looked with open mouth at the sagging, bloody shape of his employer, and at Holman who realized he probably did not look a great deal better. The woman spoke impatiently. 'George, give Mister Holman a hand. My husband won't be able to get into the house unassisted.'

'Yes, ma'am!'

George hurried forward as Holman stepped stiffly down, feeling the effects of his fight in every muscle, and in the dull ache of his shoulder with its partly healed bullet gash. He and George managed to get Sorenson to the ground but they had to support him between them. The woman had already preceded them up the steps and was holding the door open. 'To your right,' she ordered briskly. 'The second door. Put him on the bed.'

The clomp of boots sounded loud on the bare floor-boards as they maneuvered a short hallway. The second door stood open on a pleasant but impersonal room, containing a bed and chairs and a dresser. A guest room, Holman supposed, which Ruby Sorenson had steered them to because it happened to be the closest. She pulled back the spread and they lowered her husband onto the bed where he lay completely limp; he might have been dead except for the rise and fall of his breathing.

There was a muffled gasp in the doorway. A portly, gray-haired woman in an apron stared at the unconscious man and then raised her horrified glance to Ruby Sorenson. 'Ma'am!' she exclaimed 'What in the world happened?'

'It isn't serious.' The auburn-haired woman was already opening Sorenson's collar and shirt. 'Bring clean cloths and warm water from the kitchen. And antiseptic.'

The older woman—a housekeeper or cook Holman supposed—turned away on her errand, shaking her head. When the yardman had been dismissed with a nod and a brief word of thanks, Ruby Sorenson was left facing Holman over the motionless, battered figure of her husband.

'I should apologize for losing my temper, out there on the street,' Holman said gruffly. 'But I've already had a bellyful of apologizing! I tried to tell your husband I was sorry for a bad mistake I made—and he had his toughs hold me for him while he worked me over. I saw no reason to take it!' He added, 'Still, I'm sorry you had to see what I did to him.'

'Don't be,' she told him, 'because I'm not. I'm glad it happened! I really mean that,' she said earnestly, seeing his expression. I've watched this country brutalize my husband, turn him hard, and coarsen him. No woman likes to see her man beaten and made to crawl, but it will be worth it if only it teaches him humility. Perhaps this will give him back to me the way he was. At least, it's what I'm praying.'

Travis Holman frowned, extremely dubious. Still, if she wanted to believe it and could believe it strongly enough, perhaps she could even make it true. In spite of everything—in spite of the telltale bruise on her cheek, still faintly visible beneath a covering of rice powder—plainly she loved her husband, and now she had him where she wanted him, dependent upon her, and with only her to care for him.

Holman wished her luck.

* * *

Leaving her beside her husband's limp form, he walked out into the hallway and met the housekeeper returning with a steaming pan of water and towels over her arm. She looked at him sharply and said, 'You don't look too good yourself, mister. Come to the kitchen and let me wash that cut on your cheek and brush the mud out of your clothes.'

He looked down at himself. 'It will take more than that to make me presentable,' he said. 'Thanks just the same. When I get back to the hotel, I can fix myself up.'

And he went out the way he had entered, out of that opulent and unhappy household into the waning afternoon. Every muscle in his body seemed to ache.

CHAPTER TWELVE

This time he remembered to lock the door of his room and he took his gun from the holster, and when he stretched out it was on the bed beside him under his hand. He hardly expected to be bothered again, after the chastened looks he'd seen on the faces of Wade Sorenson's pair when their boss fell on his face and lay motionless in the mud; and, in fact, he wasn't. He slept undisturbed and unmoving. When he woke again, dark night was in the room and he lay exactly as he had when his head first hit the pillow.

He felt considerably better and hungry as a bear.

The evening was well advanced, but a few people were still being served in the diner a block from the hotel. The short walk stretched the stiffness out of his muscles, and he knew he had not been hurt enough to do any real damage. Even his battered skull had almost stopped aching. He took a seat at an empty table, in a corner where he could watch both door and window, and was conscious of the covert looks he got from the other customers. By now everyone in town would know about the fight in the street with Wade Sorenson. Ignoring the stares, he gave his order to the man who brought water and a plate and fistful of silverware.

He was nearly finished with his steak and potatoes when Allie Baker entered the restaurant, hesitated a moment in the doorway and then, as Holman looked up, came directly back to his table.

A gesture of her hand kept him from rising as she dropped into the chair opposite him. Her cheeks were a little flushed. He admired the way the ends of her brown hair curled up beneath the edge of her fur cap. But at the expression on her face Holman was prompted to ask, 'Is something wrong?'

'No, no,' she said quickly. 'I was looking for you. I—' Her brown eyes dropped before his. 'I went up to your room again,' she blurted, 'but I couldn't see a light under the door. I didn't know where else to look. Then I happened to notice you here, through the window.'

'I've been asleep,' he said. 'I just woke up a

little while ago.' Something must really be bothering her, he knew, for her to return to his hotel room after that first time.

The restaurant man came up, looking for an order, but Allie gave him a shake of the head and a hurried smile and he went away again. Holman sawed off another piece of steak, watching her and giving her time. She folded her hands on the edge of the table and looked at them a moment, and then lifted her eyes to him again.

'You had a fight.' He knew she was looking at the abraded swelling on his left cheek that was almost the only mark he bore. 'With Sorenson . . .'

'It didn't amount to much,' Holman said, with a shrug. 'He turned out not to be much of a fighter.'

'I know. I heard all about it. About the two men he sent to drag you out—and then how they all three tried to—' She bit her lip. 'Oh, I feel terrible about it!'

Her evident concern quickened his heartbeat a little. But he said, 'No reason to. It's finished.'

'But you don't understand!' And then the words came from her lips in a rush: 'It was my fault. All of it! I'm the one who told Sorenson everything. About losing that shipment yesterday, and about you suggesting he might have had something to do with the holdups!'

Travis Holman stared at her. 'I see,' he said

finally. But he really could see nothing at all, except that at least he had the answer to one question. He had been puzzled to know who could have informed Wade Sorenson of his suspicions. Now that he knew, it puzzled him more than ever.

He waited. 'I honestly can't tell you why I did it,' she went on miserably. 'Unless it was simply out of spite. Surely, telling Sorenson wasn't going to change his mind or make him give us another chance.' She shook her head. 'But I was so shocked when I heard the news from Burl Dempster—and angry with you, and aware of what it would mean to Frank—that when I happened to see Sorenson I blurted the whole thing. I'm very ashamed of myself. It never occurred to me that it would cost you a beating.'

'As I said,' Holman told her gruffly, 'it wasn't much of a beating. Sorenson's in much worse shape than I am, and if it brings him and his wife closer together, it may even have been all for the good.' He frowned, hesitating. 'I suppose Burl Dempster told you, it turns out I know the outlaw who's actually been hitting the shipments. He finds that pretty sinister. Do you?'

For a moment she didn't answer. 'No,' she said. 'I'm sure it was only a coincidence. Whatever you are, I don't think you could be that kind of a man.'

'Thanks for that, anyway,' Holman said in a

dry tone. He finished his coffee, pushed back his plate. Looking around he saw that the room had emptied as they sat talking. The other diners had all finished and gone, and the man was swabbing down his counter. Holman placed money beside his plate as he told the girl, ‘Looks like closing time. If I may, I’ll walk you home or to wherever you’re going.’

All right,’ she said.

*   *   *

She lived, it seemed, in a boardinghouse a block from Main Street. They walked that way almost in silence, keeping a little distance apart and not touching, except when Holman took the girl’s arm as they crossed the muddy street. But he found himself very much aware of her.

He wondered at himself. In a stormy life he had known a good many women, but mostly women for a night only, and none like Allie Baker: well-bred, honest and direct and with a clean freshness about her. Walking beside her through the dim lamplight and piled shadows of the town at night, he felt a strong sense of the emptiness of his own way of existence; a hollow core of dissatisfaction.

And then, just as they were about to turn into the side street leading to her boardinghouse, a man came reeling out into their path and Allie Baker gave a gasp and drew quickly back. Holman caught the strong smell of whiskey and saw a face in a vagrant ray of lamplight. It was the yard boss, Cash Anders. Before he could speak, Anders was by them and going on down the street, swaying slightly, his boots clomping hollowly on the boardwalk plankings.

Allie stood pressed against Holman, and he could feel her trembling slightly. 'I don't like that man!' she exclaimed. 'He frightens me.'

'He's a little drunk.'

'Drunk or sober,' she said, 'I just don't like him around! Yesterday I was walking through the yard and a brute of an ugly bay horse in one of the pens was acting up, trying to kick out the bars. It reached for me as I went by and nearly took a nip out of my arm—and Anders stood there and laughed when he saw how it scared me. He thought it was funny I nearly was bitten!'

Holman answered something, he was not sure what. His own awareness was too full, just then, of the feel of her against him. When they walked on, turning into the darker cross street, he slipped a hand beneath her arm and kept it there, and neither said anything more during the time it took to walk a short half block.

Before a house with a dark veranda and a few lighted windows, Allie Baker halted and turned to him. 'Thank you,' she said, 'for bringing me home.' She offered her hand; his own fingers seemed to tingle to the touch of it.

She went on, impulsively, 'And I want to apologize again for the trouble I caused you with Wade Sorenson. I know you did your best. It isn't fair to blame you for the way things turned out.'

Holding her hand, he said roughly, 'Everyone talks as though this fight was already lost! I don't admit that. Even if Sorenson keeps his threat to cancel his arrangement with the stage line—and he probably will—it doesn't mean we have to give up.'

Her face was a pale glimmer in the darkness, upturned to his. He heard the sudden renewal of hope in her voice. 'Do you really think there's still a chance? Oh, if there only is! If you can just do something. It's so important to Frank!'

'Damn Frank Chess!' The words were out before he knew it. His hands came up and grasped her shoulders. He spoke with angry intensity. 'He's not the only man walking around on the earth! And you know it—or you wouldn't have taken the trouble to hunt me up tonight, the way you did.'

She gasped. She laid a warding palm against his chest, but its touch only inflamed him. His arms tightened about her and he bent his head and found her mouth. Despite the push of her hand he held her closer, and under his kiss her own lips lost their stiffness and he was sure they stirred in response now he could no longer feel resistance in the palm against his chest.

When, reluctantly, he released her, she did not move away immediately. He heard her quickened breathing, and he said harshly, 'You weren't thinking about Frank Chess, just then! Don't pretend you were!'

'Why did you do that?' she exclaimed, tremulously. And then, as he was about to answer, a sound made him lift his head.

Someone was on the dark porch of the house. He came forward to the edge of the steps, where he stood staring at the man and the girl; the voice of Frank Chess sounded: 'Allie? Is that you? Mrs. Claypool said you hadn't got in yet, and I've been anxious.'

Allie drew hastily away from Holman, but she didn't speak at once, and it was Holman who said, with a hard and humorless edge to his voice, 'No need of that, Chess. I brought your girl home safe enough.'

There was no answer to that. He could feel the other's stare probing the dark. It occurred to him that Chess might not actually have seen the kiss, only the man and girl standing close together, and that perhaps he wasn't quite sure. Now he said, a little gruffly, 'Holman? I understand you had some trouble with Sorenson this afternoon.'

'Of a sort.'

'I thought I might be hearing from him myself by this time. He wasn't in his office when I went around to report this latest robbery. But it appears he must have heard the news anyway, from somebody else. I've been wondering who.'

Beside Holman, Allie stirred and he knew she was about to speak. He saw no need of her confession and forestalled it, saying quickly, 'It could have been anybody—maybe one of the yard crew. It hardly matters. Bad news always manages to find a way of getting around.'

'That's true,' Frank Chess agreed, and seemed willing to let it go. A moment passed while no one spoke. Holman, feeling the awkwardness of the silence, moved his shoulders and said, 'Well, I guess I'll say good night.'

The girl murmured something but made no effort to hold him. Frank Chess said nothing at all. Travis Holman turned away from them and started back in the direction of the main street. At a little distance, he halted for a look behind him. He was in time to see Chess open the door to the girl, her face turned up to his and his hand at her waist as be ushered her in. The door closed, the front of the house was again in darkness.

Preoccupied with his own heavy thoughts, Holman moved alone through the scattered light and shadow of the wide main street, more or less aiming for his hotel room although it was still early. The jail door stood open, and as he passed he could see Pen Shattuck seated hunched at his desk, busily writing. The deputy glanced up; he said quickly, 'Holman. You got a minute?'

'All right.'

He went in. The tiny office was equally dingy by night, though the glow of a green-shaded lamp on the desk muted its bleakness somewhat. It was chilly with the door open, but the night's clean air cut the stench from the cell block. Perhaps that was Shattuck's purpose in not closing it.

The deputy motioned him to a chair and, as his visitor seated himself, pushed aside the paper he had been writing on. He looked nervous. Peering at Holman, he fiddled with the pencil—switching ends and tapping the desk first with point and then with the chewed eraser, over and over again. He said suddenly, vehemently, 'I feel like the roof just fell on me!'

Holman raised an eyebrow. 'You?' he said with faint sarcasm. 'What's happened to *you*?'

Muscles bunched in the other's jaw. 'Damn it, I *am* supposed to represent the law here!' But under Holman's steady regard the truculence faded, and he added gruffly, 'Even if I ain't always done as well as I might at it. I won't make excuses. Between you and me, Holman, I'll admit I mainly got this job in the first place through pull. It was supposed to be an easy one, in a backwater where nothing much ever happened. But I've had the devil's own luck!'

Plainly the man had a load on his chest, and Travis Holman waited, watching him. The deputy blew out his cheeks, shaking his head as he stared moodily at the lamp. The hand that held the pencil twitched nervously. It was a blunt, square hand, the fingers tobacco-stained and saddled with black hairs across their backs, the nails habitually chewed down.

'All this trouble with the stage line!' The lawman's eyes lifted to Holman's. His tone became almost defiant. 'All right! I don't deny I been doing my best to steer clear of it. Just like I stayed clear of the fight between you and Sorenson today, out there in the street. Hell, I knew it was happening. But I figured, long as it didn't come to shooting, neither of you wanted me messing in it.'

'It's just as well you didn't,' Holman agreed briefly.

'But things are going all to blazes,' Shattuck went on bitterly, as though the other hadn't spoken. 'And now I hear I got Luke Griffin to worry about. *Luke Griffin!*' He wagged his head. 'That's a damn sight bigger mouthful than I thought I'd ever get called on to chew! I'm told you identified him. Any chance you could of made a mistake?'

'None whatever.' And since he was the law, Holman proceeded to relate as much as he thought Shattuck needed to know about the confrontation with Griffin.

When he finished, the deputy was scowling. He asked, 'How much of a gang would he have working for him?'

'I counted four, at Collier's. But I'd have no way of knowing if that's all of them.'

'Yeah . . .'

Shattuck swore and flung his pencil down on the sheet of paper half covered with his scrawl. 'I been sitting here trying to write a letter to the sheriff's office. Maybe it will do some good and get us some help in here, maybe not. Up to now, I been left to stew over this stage line trouble. I've began thinking my boss would just as soon leave me to fail at the job, so he'd have an excuse to lay me off. Well, that's politics and I got no room to complain. But, damn it!' And he slapped a palm down hard upon the desk top. 'He certainly can't ignore somebody like Luke Griffin being turned loose, right in his own county! He'll have to do something about that when he hears!'

'You know the man, I don't,' Holman said. 'Go ahead and write your letter if you think it will do any good. But the Rincon Express can't afford to wait on that.' He got to his feet, picking his hat from the desk where he had laid it. He looked down at Pen Shattuck, and saw the man's face turn red with anger.

'Or on me!' the lawman said heavily. 'That's what you're really saying, isn't it? That if I'd been worth a hoot in hell at my job, things wouldn't have got to this point . . . I never looked at it that way until yesterday,' he went on as Holman stood waiting for him to finish. 'But, until yesterday I never had outlaws riding into my town and trying to do murder, practically under my nose! It's enough to make any man take a hard look at himself. And now—Luke Griffin!'

There was little sympathy in Holman as he said coldly, 'I don't know why you're telling me this. I can't see there's anything I can do.'

'You can do this much,' the other man said, and came lunging out of his chair to face Holman squarely. The upwash of light from the lamp on the desk brought out odd planes and angles in his craggy face, and his eyes held a strange look of pleading. 'Just promise I ain't to be left out! It's little enough to ask. I'm damned if I know how to beat Griffin. Maybe, if anyone can come up with the answer, it will be you. But I'm asking at least to be allowed to have a part in it. Don't leave me out!' he said again, and his voice was tight and anxious.

For a moment Holman met his look, and something in the deputy's earnestness made him nod. 'All right,' he said gruffly. 'If anything happens, I'll try to see that you're in it.'

The deputy nodded curt thanks; it must have been a hard request to have to make. He was still standing there—an inconsequential figure, the cheap star pinned to his vest glinting in the upwash of lamplight—when

Travis Holman left him and stepped again into the night.

CHAPTER THIRTEEN

The lights of Bergman's, across the wide street, caught Holman's attention as he was about to push open the door of the hotel. They reminded him that he had unfinished business. So he turned back, tramped down the veranda steps and across the muddy stretch where he had fought it out with Sorenson a few short hours before. Entering the saloon, he found the big room empty except for Harv Bergman himself, seated at a table toward the back with a bowl of chili in front of him.

Holman walked back there, the saloon-keeper watching him come and continuing to shovel beans and meat under his villainous black mustache. A gesture with the spoon invited Holman to take one of the other chairs at the table. Chewing, Bergman studied the other's face. He said, 'Well, you come off better than I expected.'

Holman fingered the swelling on one bruised cheek. He said, 'I didn't thank you properly for your help in pulling that other pair off me. I couldn't have handled all three.'

The stocky man shrugged. 'I give 'em a little talking to after you left. Told 'em—across the muzzle of that shotgun—that I didn't want to hear of them, or any of their friends, trying to square accounts for the beating you handed Sorenson. They looked pretty scared before I finished. Don't hardly think you need to worry about them.'

'I wasn't,' Holman said briefly. 'I don't think they're the kind to act without their boss to back them up and give them orders.'

'That Sorenson!' the other grunted, wagging his bald head. 'He's an arrogant bastard!'

'He strikes me as a man outsized by his job. The company that owns the Princess has given him more of a load than he can carry. And someone that unsure of himself will do anything to keep from showing it.'

Bergman thought of that while he spooned up what was left in his bowl. The street door opened then and Burl Dempster came in. He looked around and, spotting the proprietor, called back, 'Hey! You open for business, or not?'

'Things are kind of slow,' the other answered. 'Fetch a bottle and glasses, and come on back.'

The old man seemed to know where everything was. He went around the bar and emerged with the bottle in one hand and three shot glasses in the other. As he traveled the length of the room, his bootheels rapped out echoes in the stillness. He was nearly at the table when he appeared to recognize the man who sat across from Bergman. Dempster slowed abruptly, his sour stare searching Holman's face. Then he came on, set down his burden and hauled a chair over from the neighboring table, thrust it in place and slacked into it. His mouth a tight trap, he said not a word to Holman.

Bergman had shoved his empty bowl out of the way. He picked up the bottle, uncorked it with the thrust of a splayed thumb and filled all three glasses. Holman took his and drank slowly, taking his time and feeling the welcome heat of it go to work on the remaining tensions and bruises left from the fight. Setting down the glass, he looked at Burl Dempster and found the old man staring at him.

'I've got a question that's been gnawing at me, Dempster. For what reason would a man take a sound animal out of a stage team saying it was lame, when there was nothing actually the matter with it?'

The other scowled and blinked, showing his puzzlement. 'I don't follow you. What animal you talking about, Holman?'

'Yesterday morning, just before we rolled, you'll remember Cash Anders made a switch. There was a wheeler, a bay, that he had just noticed had a bad leg. He took it out of the team and put a buckskin in its place.'

Burl Dempster made a face. 'Sure. That yaller son of a bitch! I remember.'

Holman went on: 'But Miss Baker tells me

she saw the bay not long afterward, practically tearing up the pen. It even tried to take a nip out of her arm. It could hardly have been very lame, to act like that!'

'So Anders made a mistake.'

'Perhaps. Let's think about it a minute. You've been a top whip for a good long time. I'll wager you've never forgotten any horse you ever handled—especially not when it's one that's given you the trouble you say you've had with the buckskin. Take the time before this one, the day I came along and found the stage held up and Lon McCabe shot and dying. Was the buckskin in your team then?'

The old man's fierce blue eyes were narrowly scowling. 'Damn right! Trying to turn the stage around in that narrow canyon, he all but put the whole shebang into the crick!'

'How about other times, other holdups? Can you remember? If not the buckskin, perhaps some other light-colored horse that would contrast well with the bays and blacks that seem to make up most of the company's stock.'

Unable to contain himself, Harv Bergman broke in. 'Holman, what are you reaching for?'

'I don't know. Straws, maybe. But we do know Luke Griffin is being tipped off somehow about those gold shipments. We've proved the word doesn't come from Wade Sorenson's office. That leaves no other source but the stage line itself.'

'And you think Anders could be the tip-off man?' Bergman ran a knuckle thoughtfully across his heavy mustache. 'Well,' he conceded, 'he's a surly brute.'

Holman said, 'I noticed yesterday that Griffin carries a pair of glasses on his saddle. It would be no problem for him to pick up a signal, such as an odd-colored horse in the team of any Rincon stage or freight wagon that carries a bullion shipment.'

Suddenly Burl Dempster slapped his empty tumbler on the table, with a sound that echoed sharply in the empty barn of a room. 'By God! If I was sure of—'

'But we aren't,' Holman pointed out. 'It's only a guess—and, remember what came of my guess about Wade Sorenson. Even if I should be right this time, the worst mistake we could make would be to show our hand before the draw.'

The old man scowled. 'I don't see that! Why pussyfoot around with a traitor? If Cash Anders knows where Griffin is hiding out, then it would be quickest to beat it out of him, and no better than he deserves.' He broke off as Holman shook his head. 'All right,' he grunted. 'Then what have you got in mind?'

Travis Holman told his ideas, feeling no reluctance about talking in front of Bergman. The saloon man had done him more than one favor, and Holman had begun to look on him as a trustworthy, personal friend. The others heard him out in silence, and it was Bergman who wagged his bald head and said solemnly, 'It might work.'

Burl Dempster looked dubious. 'You think we might be rushing things? Another shipment—this soon? I don't imagine Luke Griffin's any fool. After two holdups inside a week, he just might be suspicious.'

'On the other hand,' Travis Holman pointed out, 'he doesn't know how desperate we may be. Anyway, it's a risk we have to take. If we wait, there's too good a chance of his learning of the break with Sorenson—and then it will be too late.'

The old man pursed his lips. 'I guess you're right,' he agreed, though he sounded reluctant. 'So it has to be tomorrow.'

Depending, of course, on Frank Chess. It's his decision.' Holman pushed back his chair, rose. 'I'll go see what he says. I also want to talk to Pen Shattuck.'

Shattuck!' Dempster spoke the deputy's name as though it tasted bad. 'Who needs *him?*'

'I promised the man if there was any action he'd have a chance to be in it.'

'I'd like to be in it,' Harv Bergman said abruptly, and as they both looked at him in surprise, he continued, 'For a fact! This business has gone on long enough. I know of a couple other guys would be glad to lend a hand in winding it up if you can use them.'

'Who, for instance?' Burl Dempster demanded. Bergman gave a pair of names that meant nothing to Holman, but they got Dempster's nod of approval. 'Both good men.'

'Get them!' Holman told the saloon man. 'I'll leave it for you and Dempster to name the time and place where we'll pick you up. Against Griffin's outfit, we can use all the help we're able to get.'

*   *   *

A ground fog had burned away with the rising of the sun, leaving the freight yard's dirt streaked black with moisture. But anyone observing Burl Dempster, where he leaned against a wheel of a big canvas top freight wagon and toyed idly with the coils of his bullwhip, might have thought he found no pleasure in the fresh morning that, for once, carried no trace of sulfur fumes from the smelter workings. To all appearance he was glum, at loose ends, wholly despondent. Travis Holman, approaching through the gate in the high fence, thought, *I just hope he isn't carrying it too far.*

As he came up, the old driver shot him a sour look beneath the thickets of his brows, returned his greeting with no more than a nod. Halting, Holman asked quietly, 'Where is he?'

'Careful!' Dempster grunted. 'He's lookin' at you. From the door of the stable, yonder.'

Holman made a casual half turn to put an elbow on a spoke of the big wheel. This swung him to face the stable entrance, and he saw Cash Anders. The yard boss was giving orders to one of his pair of helpers, who with manure fork and wheelbarrow had been given the job of cleaning out the stalls. Now Anders stared boldly across the yard at Holman, and the latter knew he didn't imagine the mocking look of satisfaction on his swarthy face.

'Look at him!' Burl Dempster growled under his breath. 'Standing there sneering at us! I'd like to use this on the son of a bitch!' And he flicked the whip, with a snap like a gunshot that raised a tawny spurt of dust.

'Is this the wagon we're going to use?' Holman asked. At the other's nod, he pushed away from the wheel, adding, 'Everything appears set, then. I'll go see Frank Chess and start things rolling.'

The old man nodded, looking as gloomy as ever; a picture of a man contemplating the end of his job, and the failure of the company he worked for. Without a second glance at Anders, Holman headed at an angle across the yard and, unhurriedly, up the steps to the side door.

On entering, he sensed at once that he had interrupted something. Frank Chess stood at the file cabinet and Allie Baker sat at the work table, and they both appeared upset. The girl's face was white. As the door opened she was saying, 'Frank! Please!' She broke off, glancing at Holman and quickly away again. He had not seen her since that moment before her house, the night before. Looking at her profile, at the mouth that he had kissed, he wondered what she thought of it now—and of him.

But other matters were pressing. Turning to Chess, he said, 'If you're ready, we may as well start.'

'Ready,' Chess said, sliding shut the drawer of the file. 'I'll call Anders in.' To Allie he said, 'You've got the letter?'

She indicated wordlessly a sealed envelope that lay on the work table, her whole manner troubled and disapproving. Chess nodded and went past Holman to the side door and, opening it, called across the yard to Cash Anders. They waited, all of them tense, as they heard the man's boots grate the drying mud and tromp the steps. Anders's lean, hump-shouldered figure filled the doorway.

'Yeah?' he said.

Frank Chess told him, 'I have a chore for you. This letter must go to Wade Sorenson's office at the mine.'

'You want me to take it?' Handed the envelope, Anders looked at it scowling. 'Since when have I become a messenger boy? That ain't part of my job.'

'It is if I say so!' Chess answered, too curtly. He caught Holman's warning and went on, in a more placating tone, 'I don't think there's anything in the yard that needs your attention this morning, and it's really important that the letter be delivered. I'd rather not trust it to one of the yardmen.'

Still frowning, Anders objected, 'Sorenson might not be at his office. Seems I heard he was in bed, laid up.' His muddy stare stabbed accusingly at Holman as he said it.

'Then if you don't find him, try his home,' Chess said. 'I know it's a nuisance, and I'm sorry to have to ask you. There's no reason for you to hurry about reporting back. We're rather at a standstill here. Take the rest of the morning if you like.'

Anders shrugged. With the letter in his hand he ran his stare deliberately from Chess to Holman, and then to the girl. Then, turning away, he shoved the envelope into a pocket of his denim jacket and slammed the door after him.

'So much for that,' Frank Chess said.

'Let's hope he swallowed it.'

The other flashed him a look. 'Why shouldn't he? It was perfectly legitimate. The letter *does* have to reach Sorenson. He still hasn't had an official report of the loss of that last shipment.' He turned abruptly to a closet, opened it and took out a hat and jacket. From the nail he lifted down a shell belt and holster that did not look as though they had ever seen use. The cherrywood grips of the six-shooter in the holster were unpolished and undarkened by handling; the blueing of the metal was still new.

Rather awkwardly he hitched the belt into place about his middle and fumbled at the buckle. There was a sound from Allie Baker. Looking at her, Travis Holman saw the anguish in her face and thought he knew what they had been quarreling about when he walked into the office. She said, pleading, 'Frank! Do you have to—?'

'Yes!' he told her bluntly. 'If this isn't my concern, then I don't know whose it is. One man has already been killed trying to protect my stage line. I have no right to send anyone out to face a thing I'm not willing to meet myself!'

There was the sound of a horse in the yard outside. Through the window at his elbow, Holman saw Cash Anders in the saddle and riding out under the high crossbar of the yard gate. 'There he goes,' Frank Chess said. 'Time for us to be moving.'

Holman nodded. 'I'll give Burl Dempster the word.'

CHAPTER FOURTEEN

There was no need to alert Burl Dempster. Just like the people in the office, he had been waiting for Cash Anders's departure. When

Holman came out he was already approaching the stock pens at a run, harness slung across his shoulder.

He summoned Holman with a jerk of the head. 'You gonna give me a hand with this yaller son of a bitch? I'd hate to lose my temper and put a bullet between his eyes before we even get him into the traces!' He added, 'I see Anders rose to the bait. I still can't help thinking we'd done better to knock him in the head and leave him tied up someplace. I know I'd feel better, knowing he was where he couldn't do any more mischief!'

'Chess insisted on handling it this way,' Holman said. 'He's not convinced, and even if Anders is guilty, he thinks it's best not to let on we know.'

'He's the boss,' the old man grunted.

Allie Baker, watching these preparations from a window of the office, anxiously worried her lower lip as she looked at the two men who had become the most important in her life. Travis Holman and Frank Chess. So very different, those two, from such different backgrounds; one hardened and tempered by the violence of his life, the other gentler by nature but with a steadiness and a stubborn will of his own. Seeing them like this, knowing the danger they would soon be facing, she knew that the thought of anything happening to either one was more than she could bear.

So engrossed was she in her thoughts that

she failed to hear the street door open. But a boot kicked it shut with a slam, and she came about quickly, and then could only stare as Cash Anders crossed the room toward her. He should have been on his way to the Princess Mine. He couldn't possibly have completed his mission in this short a time. Seeing the scowl on his lean, black-stubbled cheeks she stammered, 'Is—is something wrong?'

Anders had already searched the room with his muddy stare. He demanded, 'Where is he? Where's Chess?'

'But you were supposed to be—'

'Where's Chess, damn him!'

Anders shoved open the partition gate. As he did so, Allie saw the paper crumpled in his hand and recognized it. 'That's the letter for Mr. Sorenson. You *opened* it!'

'Sure I opened it! And I want to know what the hell he's hinting at, about me!'

'Why, I copied the letter. It doesn't even mention you.'

'Oh, no?' the man retorted. 'Just listen!' He referred to the paper and read the words aloud, spitting them out: 'I want to apologize for thinking you might have been criminally involved in some way. It begins to appear I should have looked closer to home.' His eyes pinned her. 'Maybe you can explain that!'

As she tried to find words, the sound reached them of a wagon rolling into motion, out in the hard-backed yard. Anders whipped his head around. 'Somebody's taking out a wagon!' he exclaimed. 'What the hell, there's none scheduled.' He strode to the window, pushing Allie aside, but not before she had had a glimpse of the canvas-topped rig heading for the gate with Burl Dempster on the seat, and Travis Holman riding his dun horse alongside. She saw the buckskin hitched to the wagon, in harness with a heavy-shouldered black, and already trying to act up as it felt the slap of the reins across its rump.

Then the wagon had vanished through the gate, and Cash Anders's face took on a dark and terrible anger. The hand that held the letter tightened to a fist. He swore fiercely as he turned from the window—and Allie Baker, at the weapons rack, brought up the rifle she had snatched from it. With trembling hands she worked the lever and then braced the butt of it against her hip, the muzzle pointed at the man's chest.

A grunt of shock broke from Cash Anders. He halted in mid-stride. The letter dropped from his hand, forgotten.

'Put that up!' he ordered harshly.

Her face so pale that the freckles on her nose stood out clearly, Allie shook her head. She saw Anders's hand move an inch or two nearer the gun in his hip holster, and her mouth went dry. He hadn't been wearing a gun when he left the office earlier. But he didn't seem ready to touch it now. Eyes speculative, he considered the weapon that threatened him. 'It ain't loaded,' he said.

'You want to take a chance?' Her finger was on the trigger, her hand tight on the action. When Anders still hesitated, she told him hotly, 'Frank never accused you of anything in his letter. It was your own guilty conscience! I know if I had any doubts before, they're gone now!'

But he didn't seem inclined to make any further protests of innocence. 'What tipped him off to me?' he demanded. 'Or maybe it was Holman's idea?'

'Yes!' she flung at him. 'Travis Holman's the one who finally saw through you.' Contempt made her voice tremble. 'Your conscience *should* bother you. To help destroy a man who's done as much for you as Frank Chess has—putting you in charge of all his stock and equipment, paying you top wages and trusting you.'

Cash Anders shrugged heavy shoulders. 'The hell with that! A job's nothing more than a job. He hired me, he took his chances. Now take that damn thing off me!'

'So you can go to Luke Griffin and warn him about the wagon?' She shook her head firmly. 'You're going to stay right where you are!'

She had never met such cold hatred as she saw staring from those hooded eyes. They seemed to burn into her own, and she felt her knees shaking. She told herself, fiercely, *You little goose! Whatever you do, you're not going to faint!* The man's heavy breathing, and the chatter of a tin clock on a shelf, alone broke the stillness. How long, she wondered desperately, could she hold him?

She thought of calling for help, but the only ones within possible sound of her voice would be the two yardmen. In her near state of shock, she couldn't bring herself to cross the short distance to the side door. Besides, those men had been Anders's helpers; horrible doubts assailed her—were they really to be trusted?

But holding the heavy rifle steady was telling on her. Her arms were beginning to ache, and her legs were shaking slightly: Just to see Cash Anders standing there studying her was unnerving. She had to clear her throat before she could speak. 'We could be here quite awhile. I'd rather you were sitting down.' Once she had him settled she could take a seat herself, perhaps rest her arms by propping the rifle barrel on the table's edge.

Anders seemed to debate whether to pay any attention to the command. Apparently her firmness of manner decided him. With a last killing look, he turned away. A chair stood against the deal table that filled much of the space here behind the partition. He jerked it out and turned it, as though to seat himself—and then, with a blinding suddenness, whipped the chair up and flung it straight at her.

Allie stifled a cry as she twisted aside, out of the way. It crashed into the wall beside her, and then Anders was upon her and his big hand made a sharp, sweeping arc and took her on the side of the head. She was flung around; the rifle was wrenched from her grasp. And then her head struck an edge of the weapons rack, blackness engulfed her and she fell into it.

Cash Anders stood over the unconscious girl, breathing bard, holding the captured rifle by its barrel. His mouth worked; he spat a single word: 'Bitch!'

He immediately forgot her in the press of more urgent matters. A glance through the window showed that the compound was idle; neither of the yard men appeared to have heard anything of what happened within the office, and anyway they would probably not have interfered. They were nothing more than bindlestiffs, taking his orders and his heavy-handed blows for fifty cents a day and a bottle of booze to split between them.

Anders calculated the time he had been delayed and swore luridly. Too late now, probably, to overtake the wagon. Besides, that would mean coming to grips with Travis Holman himself, something Cash Anders had no particular stomach for. One thing was clear, though—Luke Griffin must somehow be warned, before he rose to the bait of that harmless appearing wagon.

Starting for the street door, Anders realized he still held the rifle he had taken from the girl. He had one on his saddle, he didn't need this. He tossed it onto the deal table, where it landed with a clatter. Without another glance at Allie Baker's crumpled form, he pushed through the partition gate and hurried out to his horse waiting in front of the office. He flung himself into the saddle and drummed the animal with his heels, sending it into a leaping start. He took the south road, mud spurting under the animal's shoes.

CHAPTER FIFTEEN

Burl Dempster raised dust with a vicious slap of the rein against the buckskin wheeler's rump and showed tobacco-stained teeth in a snarl as the animal tossed its ugly head. 'That damned yaller judas hoss!' he growled. 'I always knew there was something wrong with him. I should of plugged him one of them times when I was tempted!'

Travis Holman, pacing his dun horse alongside the slowly moving wagon, swallowed a smile. 'He's not to blame for the color of his hide, or the purpose he was used for.'

The old man grunted something and spat. 'You know,' he said after a few further turns of the big wheels, 'ever since you told me about them damned field glasses, I've had the feeling somebody's looking down the back of my neck!' He tilted a nervous glance toward the rise of rock and timber, crowding above the stage road's ruts. 'Those bastards must have a lookout posted around the clock, with an eye always out for any of our rigs.'

'Only during the morning, probably,' Holman said. 'It being a full day's haul to Seven Pines, they would know you'd be getting an early start any time you made a run.'

'If we'd just realized it,' the old man grumbled, 'we could have crossed 'em up by making a night run now and then. Well, a man can always figure, too late, what he *should* have done.'

'They'd have worked out something else, then.'

'I don't doubt!' After a few minutes of silence, broken by the slam and protest of timbers, the grind of tires and the plodding of the horses, Dempster said impatiently, 'I just wish they'd do something to bring this to a head! When they do,' he added, squinting against the sun at the man on the horse, 'you realize you're gonna be their prime target? You're just inviting the first bullet to dump you off of that saddle, once they open the ball!'

That was so unpleasantly obvious that Holman didn't bother to answer, though he could have pointed out that the bait would not have been complete without him. Luke Griffin might not have believed a completely unguarded wagon. He might even have guessed a trap. But the sight of Travis Holman accompanying it should almost certainly bring him. Even more important, he was pretty sure to bring all his men with him, expecting a fight.

Travis Holman was not interested in halfway measures. This might be the last chance at them, and he wanted the whole gang.

A quarter mile ahead, the road took a blind twist and dipped from sight around a timbered hump of ground. Holman had been eyeing it narrowly. Now he raised his glance to the ridge above them. He told Dempster, 'I see a likely spot for a look. Keep rolling. I'll join you beyond that hump.'

Not waiting for an answer he reined in, let the wagon roll past as he checked the canvas that was pulled tight over the bows and at the rear. He then crossed the road behind the rig and sent his horse up into the rock and scrub timber.

From the ledge he had seen, there was a ranging view over the country ahead. It looked harmless enough: range and timberland, dappled with cloud shadow, moisture from the recent rains steaming under the high morning sun. Across this the stage road looped like a brown ribbon, empty of traffic. Now the slowly lumbering wagon came into view. He sat and watched it for a moment as it moved away from him, with nothing about it to hint that under its mud-stained canvas there could be anything of interest to an outfit of looters. So innocent and peaceful did the entire scene appear that Travis Holman—a restless man by nature—began to feel the roweling of impatience, and a first strong stirring of doubt.

Perhaps he had guessed wrong once again. Perhaps this whole maneuver was a waste of time. It would mean he had failed in his job here, and the Rincon Express had lost the final gamble.

With an angry shake of the head, he lifted the reins to ride down off his perch—and then quickly checked again. For he had seen something, a mere flicker of movement in the thick nap of timber stretching away from this high point. He waited with held breath, and where the trees thinned briefly he saw it again: a group of horsemen, riding two abreast across a clearing as they threaded their way down the rough slope toward the road. They were gone quickly enough, but they left Travis Holman with a tingling sense of justification.

A minute longer he stayed where he was, estimating the riders' course and the speed of the wagon rolling unawares toward the point where they would spike the road. Afterward he sent the dun forward, picking his own way down the slant with the pine tree heads wheeling across the spring sky and slick rock sliding under the animal's hoofs.

He had still some distance to travel when the first shot sounded, startlingly, somewhere beyond the screen of timber that hemmed him in.

That shot had come from a rifle in the hands of a horseman who had suddenly appeared a dozen feet ahead of Burl Dempster. Fired, as a warning, the bullet sang past his head and the muzzle blast set the buckskin horse plunging wildly in the harness. Dempster swore and fought to settle it, the wagon slewing to an odd angle before he got everything under control. He sat there glowering blackly at the rifle that was pointed now directly at his chest.

The man who held it was Luke Griffin. He looked into the cold eyes, in the narrow, hawklike face, and he swallowed back the lump of terror that clogged his throat. He was damned if he would show this man any trace of fear, not even when other horsemen spilled out of the timber to join him, all openly carrying drawn guns.

Griffin, for his part, had at once seen something wrong. He demanded harshly, 'Where'd Holman get to? And don't lie to me. He was with you not five minutes ago.'

The old man shrugged. 'Said something about his horse picked up a stone. I reckon he dropped back to see to it.'

Luke Griffin promptly barked an order. 'Sid! You and a couple of the boys go look for him. Don't give him the first shot.'

'Don't worry about that!' The towheaded outlaw, Sid Flagg, spoke a couple of names, and those he had summoned followed as he spurred past the stalled wagon. The remaining pair looked to their chief for orders.

Griffin's stare settled again on Burl Dempster. 'What's in the wagon?'

'Nothin'!' He forced a contemptuous defiance into his voice. 'You drawn a blank this time, damn you. You already got it all. I'm hauling empty.'

'You expect me to believe that? With Holman himself riding guard?' Griffin waved his men forward with a gesture of the rifle barrel. 'Take a look.'

Burl Dempster's breath caught in his throat as they dismounted to carry out their order. With that rifle centered on him, he could do nothing. His muscles tensed as he caught a sound of movement in the wagon behind him—the scrape of a boot . . .

Suddenly canvas was pushed aside, the metal of a gun barrel rang against wood. A voice, high-pitched and shaking with tension, called out: 'This is the law! I'll give you five seconds to surrender!'

He groaned. That damned fool of a deputy. What did he have in his head for brains, to be standing on ceremony at a time like this, giving the whole play away when he should have just started shooting! And then the shooting *did* start, a quick and startling explosion of sound as a half dozen guns began at once.

Someone cried out in pain, a horse squealed shrilly. At once Burl Dempster was forgotten. Seeing his chance as Luke Griffin spurred to join his men at the wagon, he hastily dropped the lines and groped beneath the seat for the shotgun he'd stowed there. As his hand closed on the metal tube he was making a lunge for the high wheel, and he took an unceremonious, headlong dive across it, desperately putting the wagon between him and the outlaws.

He landed on back and shoulders, the hard ground driving the wind out of him. For an instant he was left dazed with pain, but he forced himself to roll over onto his belly and then crawl hurriedly behind the wheel, dragging the shotgun to him. From there, he peered between the spokes at the confusion of activity beyond.

His vision was limited but he could see one of the raiders on his face in the road ruts, a lifeless sprawl. Anxious to see more, he risked being crushed by a wheel of his own wagon as he hitched himself forward on his elbows, underneath the rig itself. The skittish team was acting up, terrified by the gunfire; the wagon lurched crazily. And now the ground began to shake to a drum of galloping horses. Twisting for a look to the rear, he glimpsed Sid Flagg and the pair who had ridden off with him to hunt for Travis Holman.

Alerted by the firing, they were coming back fast and shooting as they came, directing their fire into the wagon's canvas. Dempster swore. *Damn that Holman!* This had all been his idea: Set a trap and lure Griffin into it. Now the trap had sprung, and the thing had turned into a melee, and it looked like everybody was going to get killed—and just where was the great Travis Holman?

In that moment one of those oncoming horses took a bullet and went down in a crashing, skidding plunge. Dempster winced when he saw its rider trapped by his stirrup and pinned as the animal's weight landed full on top of him. Then Dempster saw Holman, in the edge of the timber, holding the dun steady under him while his smoking gun fired again.

Again he found a target; a second outlaw went spinning out of the saddle, and his horse collided with Sid Flagg's animal just as the blond outlaw was about to throw down for a try at Holman. Hurled off balance in mid-stride, the animal went up on its hind legs and spun clear around, nearly thrown off its feet before it could come solidly to earth again.

Flagg never got off his shot, for Holman fired again and Dempster, watching under the wagon, saw Flagg flung violently sideward as the bullet struck him.

Holman had fired just three bullets and scored every time! Suddenly Flagg seemed to have faced all of that kind of shooting he wanted. He had managed to keep his seat. Having got the horse under a semblance of control, he wrenched the reins wildly, spurs flailing. Burl Dempster had a glimpse of the blond outlaw's distorted features, before a couple of leaps by the frenzied animal carried him around the rear end of the wagon. That put the rig between him and Holman's deadly gun, but Flagg had no more thought of fighting. He kept going, the horse settling to an all-out run.

Too late Dempster remembered he had a weapon of his own. He slowed around on his belly, triggered a blast of the shotgun in the outlaw's wake but knew it was wasted. Then the fugitive had vanished, leaving the boom of the shotgun ringing in his ears. As this faded, he realized silence had settled upon the wagon, broken only by the steady, monotonous cursing of someone with a bullet wound. The battle was over.

* * *

With some distance behind him, Sid Flagg eased out of his first pell-mell rush and pulled in behind a screen of brush, where his horse could blow while he checked for sign of pursuit. He also needed a look at his leg. Holman's bullet had sliced across the muscle at the top of his thigh and it was bleeding so badly it scared him; the searing pain seemed less important. With shaking hands, he ripped off his neckcloth and stuffed it into the rip in his trouser leg, trying to staunch the flow.

Drawing his six-shooter, then, he took a look back at his trail. He was sweating.

The sound of a shoe iron scraping rock came from somewhere to the right. His head whipped around and he almost crimped off a bullet before he recognized Luke Griffin, walking his own horse out from behind a clump of boulders. Blinking pale red-rimmed eyes, Flagg lowered the gun as the other joined him. He said huskily, 'I almost put a slug in you. What the hell are you doing here?'

'Same as you're doing,' Griffin answered coldly. 'Saving my hide. I heard you behind me. I was waiting to see who it was.'

Flagg let out his breath in a ragged explosion. 'Are we the only ones who made it? God! We really walked into a hailstorm, back there!'

'We walked into a trap.'

'That Holman!' The knuckles that clutched the gun showed white under the matting of blond fur. 'Chief, I told you at Collier's station you should have let me plug him, while we had the chance!'

'The man I want in front of my sights,' Griffin said, 'is the traitor who sold us out to him.'

'Anders?'

The other nodded bitterly. His hawkish

features showed the controlled ferment of rage within. 'The minute I spotted the rig through the glasses, I had a feeling somehow it was wrong. But I never really thought he'd dare to cross me.'

'Looks like he's safe enough,' the blond man said with a shrug. 'There ain't much you can do to him. One thing you can count on, the bastard's certainly going to make sure you never meet up with him again.'

'He can't be that careful!' Luke Griffin retorted. 'I proved to Holman I never forget a favor—but, neither does any man cross me and get away with it. Sooner or later, I'll pay Cash Anders off for this.' And looking into those cold eyes, Sid Flagg could believe it.

'But this is *now*,' the blond man said. 'The gang's shot to hell, only the two of us left.'

'And only two of us to split the gold,' Griffin reminded him, with an indifference that curdled his blood a little. 'Let's go pack it up and clear out of this country. Looks like our game here is over.'

'We got to do something about my leg,' Sid Flagg exclaimed. 'Before I bleed dry.'

Luke Griffin glanced at the soaked trouser leg, dismissed it with a shrug as he picked up the reins. 'You're all right. We'll work on it when we get to the cabin. Come along.'

He turned his horse and touched it with the spur. Shaken and frightened at his hurt, Sid Flagg had no choice but to follow.

CHAPTER SIXTEEN

It was a familiar pattern. After the excitement of battle, after the guns had quit, came the letdown and the unpleasant task of tallying the score. The dun was still wild-eyed and trembling, ready to bolt like the horses of the raiders. Travis Holman led it by the reins as he walked from one body to another, checking them for signs of life. He had his gun ready but there was no need of it. All four outlaws were dead.

But the one he wanted was missing. Pouching his gun, finally, Holman looked up to find Burl Dempster standing beside him. He shook his head. 'Luke Griffin's not here.'

'He was,' the old man said. 'So he got away in the confusion. Also, that yaller-haired one, that Flagg. I think you put a bullet in him, though. You done some damn good shooting.' He added, 'The same with this whole operation. I can see how you had it figured right, all down the line.' There was definite and ungrudging respect in the old fellow's manner, and Holman knew he had scored at least one victory.

He said only, 'It isn't good enough. Griffin got away.' And he turned back to see how it was with the men at the wagon.

Limping after him, Dempster rubbed a

shoulder and grumbled half to himself, 'I'm too old for fool stunts like divin' off a wagon like that. I ought to know better. I could cripple myself for—' His complaining trailed off as they approached the rig.

Part of those who had sprung the trap on Luke Griffin were standing about the wagon, holding their guns and wearing dazed expressions as though not even yet sure it was over. Holman saw the grim look on Harv Bergman's face and demanded sharply, 'Who got hurt?'

The saloon owner answered in a voice turned husky by the aftermath of violence. 'Pen Shattuck is bleeding; I don't think it's serious. But Frank Chess took a bad one.'

Quickly, Holman shoved past. The canvas had been pulled up and he could see Chess lying on his back, apparently unconscious. Reaching across the side of the wagon box, he pulled open the front of the bloodstained coat. Someone had tried to improvise a compress for the chest wound, high in the right side. Holman considered it silently, then turned to Shattuck who sat clutching a red-soaked arm against him.

The deputy sheriff's face was drained of color, his eyes glazed with shock. When Holman dropped a hand upon his unhurt shoulder, he lifted his head and asked unsteadily, 'Did—did we do all right?'

'We did fine,' Holman assured him. 'Just

hang on and we'll get you to the doctor.' Turning to Burl Dempster, he said, 'Don't waste any time. Not with that hole Frank Chess has in him. I don't like the looks of it.'

'We're practically on our way.'

The old driver moved spryly enough, clambering up to his seat. Holman flipped the reins across the dun's back and swung astride, muscles protesting a little—he could still feel some of the effects of his bout with Wade Sorenson. Remembering the empty shells in his gun he drew it and punched them out and was thumbing fresh cartridges from his belt when he saw Bergman watching him. 'You're not going with us?' the saloon man said.

'The job's not finished.'

'Maybe, if you could catch me up one of those horses the raiders lost . . .'

Travis Holman considered him a long moment, then shook his head. Bergman was game but he was really no fighter, and he didn't have much of the look of a horseman. 'I can't take the time,' Holman said. 'I appreciate the offer, but this is my job.'

He thought Bergman looked relieved to have his help refused. Actually, an amateur would only get in the way. He dropped his loaded gun into the holster and kicked the dun into motion.

He was following a man who had been too intent on escaping from the scene of a debacle to worry about the trail he left. It was no great task to follow, and presently it joined sign of a second horseman whom he judged to be Luke Griffin himself. There were only the two of them, and that made it look as though Griffin had held nothing in reserve. He'd ridden to intercept the wagon with every one of his men, and all but himself and Flagg were dead.

On getting into rougher country, there seemed to have been some attempt to lose the trail. Once Travis Holman hesitated, unsure of the route to take and driven by impatience, he glimpsed what could only be a smear of blood on a rough rock face. Leaning from the saddle to touch it, he found it still faintly damp. So he had not been wrong to think he had managed to tag Sid Flagg with a bullet. Passing this rock, Flagg had scraped it with his blood-drenched trouser leg, giving his pursuer the bearing he needed. From that moment, even as the way grew progressively rougher and the dun began to show signs of tiring, there was no real danger again of Holman's losing the scent.

The sign led him up through a narrow-walled ravine that was well-marked with travel. Without any warning, this leveled out upon the floor of a pocket containing a few acres of timber and grass, and surrounded by granite faces that had crumbled away at one place, creating a jackstraw tumble of long dead timber and broken boulders. There was a glint of water, collected from a spring. And at the far side of this sheltered cup, Holman saw a cabin.

It was built of logs gone gray with time, with a shake roof and a mud chimney and shuttered windows. A couple of corrals were newer, made from peeled poles that still showed yellow bright where the bark had been removed. When the bray of a mule rang like a bugle in the stillness, Travis Holman suddenly remembered he was perfectly visible where he had reined in, at the mouth of the draw which served as the exit from the hideout. With a hurried reflex, he drew aside into a clump of jack pine and swung to earth.

He could only hope he had moved in time to keep from being seen by those over at the cabin.

Drawing his gun, he left his horse and started forward, keeping to the fringe of pine that rimmed the bottom of the cup. This gave him cover but it also limited his vision, so that he traveled blind and got no more than a glimpse or two of the cabin until he was a bare fifty yards from it. There, the scrub growth fell back, and suddenly there was open ground ahead of him, spotted by a few boulders and occasional clumps of brush.

Now he could make out the black mouth of a mine adit, framed in ancient timbers, that scarred the barren slope behind the cabin. That and a pile of old tailings told the story: At one time or other this had been some lonely miner's hole up. Someone had built the cabin and had lived there for a season or two while he worked at his claim, though it didn't look as though it could ever have been a particularly rich one. As with so many such workings, the vein had pinched out or been lost in country rock when the shaft hit a fault line. The miner would have stayed on for a while, hoping and hunting. Eventually he would have packed up and moved on to hunt elsewhere, leaving his cabin to stand deserted and forgotten.

Forgotten—until Luke Griffin came looking for a base of operations, found it, and took it over.

There was movement in one of the corrals; he counted three mules penned inside it. Near the cabin, a pair of saddled horses stood with heads drooping, as though exhausted. He was certain Sid Flagg had ridden one of them at the holdup. That spelled but one thing. The pair he sought were either in the cabin, or somewhere near.

The one window he could see, and the open door, told him nothing of what was happening within. There was a dead silence, except for the buzz of insects in the afternoon heat that collected in this forgotten pocket. Even the mules over in the corral were still. Holman watched the drooping horses as they switched tails at the flies, and one shifted its weight and stomped fretfully. It seemed foolhardy to approach directly toward the shack and those two blank openings. He debated whether the best bet would be to make a circle, perhaps come up beyond the corrals and work in closer that way, or simply wait and try to pick them off as they came back for their horses.

Behind him then, a voice spoke without warning. 'Don't move, Holman! My gun's aimed at the back of your neck.'

He froze, the breath caught in his throat. He was hopelessly caught and knew it. 'All right,' he said roughly.

'No need to turn around,' the voice said. 'Not yet. Just toss that gun on the ground behind you, and then stand hitched.' It would have been suicide to do anything else. With a shrug, Holman reached back and let the gun fall. A twig snapped under boot leather as someone came toward him, stepping cautiously. 'All right,' he was ordered. 'Now lift your hands, and turn—slow!'

He had already recognized the voice, and so felt no surprise when be came around to discover Cash Anders facing over a leveled gun barrel. Anders had picked up Holman's six-shooter, and now he tossed this away into the brush. He looked tense, nerves tight; Holman could see the sweat shining on his cheeks as the yard boss approached and, still keeping him covered, reached out his free hand to slap the pockets of the prisoner's coat. Flipping the coat open, he seemed to satisfy himself that the other man had no further weapon. He stepped back. His face held triumph but he was nervous, too.

Holman saw another horse tethered a little distance back in the trees, its sweat-darkened hide dappled by the shadow of pine branches overhead. A carbine stood in the saddle scabbard. Cash Anders said harshly, 'Had I been a better rifle shot I could have knocked you off your bronc as soon as you come through the gate.'

Holman coldly returned his stare. 'I guess you know that we figured out the signal. But did you know your treachery had put a bullet into Frank Chess? He may be dead from it by this time.'

He thought the muddy eyes flickered uncomfortably, but Anders shrugged. 'I ain't heard anything,' he mumbled. 'I only got here a minute or two ahead of you. But I think Sid and Luke are in the cabin.' He gestured with the gun barrel. 'Start walking. They're going to be real interested when they see what I'm bringing them!'

There was no arguing with a drawn gun. Sweating a little himself now, Holman only hoped the man could control the nervous pressure of his finger on the trigger. He moved carefully, so as to give no excuse for alarm as he let himself be herded into the open. With Anders close on his heels he began the uneasy approach to the silent cabin.

The first dozen yards they crossed, he could still see no evidence of life within the shack, only the two saddled horses standing a little distance away. The sun bore down; the stillness lay heavy and was broken only by the scrape of their own boots on rock rubble, as they started a slight climb toward the place where the cabin stood.

And then something moved within the darkness beyond the open door, swam into clearer view and became the figure of a man with a rifle in his hands.

It was Luke Griffin. He stood in the opening, watching the approaching pair. Then, deliberately, he raised the rifle and bent his head over the sights. And, in horror, Travis Holman realized the man was going to shoot! There was no time to think. Caught between the rifle and the menace of a six-shooter at his back, he acted on a desperate instinct for survival simply flinging himself to one side, hardly expecting to be alive when he hit the ground.

CHAPTER SEVENTEEN

He struck hard, rolling.

By some miracle, the six-gun at his back did not go off. But the rifle cracked flatly almost in the instant that he made his move. He heard a cry of alarm: 'Luke! Damn it, you nearly got me that time. This is Cash Anders.'

And Luke Griffin's reply: 'Yeah, I see who it is, you bastard!' And the rifle spoke again. Holman thought he actually heard the impact of lead striking flesh and bone. There was a sound of agony, quickly broken off, and a body struck the ground. Griffin shouted, 'Nobody sells me out!'

None of it made sense. Still slightly dazed, Travis Holman raised his head. He had half rolled, half slid into a slight hollow. Whether it was deep enough to give any protection from a rifle, he had no way of knowing. He hugged the earth, as flat as he could make himself. His shoulder muscles bunched as the rifle sounded a third time, and dirt and rock fragments showered him.

Griffin tried again with no better success. Still, he had Travis Holman pinned down with his face pressed against the gritty soil, unable to move and without any kind of weapon.

He heard his own name, a painful whisper: *'Holman!'* Cautiously he turned his head to look at Cash Anders sprawled a half dozen feet away, where Griffin's rifle had dropped him. The muddy eyes were wide, and staring; blood ran from his slack mouth into the dirt. He spoke with an effort, the words hardly reaching the short distance. 'Can you hear me?'

'I hear you.'

'I'm done for. I'm all shot up inside. Damn him—*why*?'

He sought an answer in Holman's face. The latter could only shake his head. 'I suppose you'll never know,' he said. 'Somehow he seems to think you double-crossed him.'

Anders's breath was coming fast and shallow now, fluttering his lips, spraying out a foam of bloody spittle. Obviously he didn't have long. But he found his voice again, and there was a breathless urgency behind it. 'The gold, from the Princess—that I helped him steal . . . You listening, Holman?'

'Yes.'

'That's what you're after, ain't it? Well, it's all there, stored in that old mine shaft on the slope behind the cabin. Don't let him have it, Holman!' The man's face contorted in a spasm of agony. 'He had no reason to do this. I never sold him out!'

Holman thought he could all but see the life slowly ebbing from that other face. Inches from his outflung hand lay the gun the yard boss had dropped when he fell with Griffin's bullet in him. Holman called to him: 'Anders! The gun—pick it up and toss it to me. Make an effort!'

He was not even sure his words had got through. But then he saw a feeble movement of the slack fingers. They stirred, fumbled in the dirt, groping for the weapon. They found it—and in the next instant, twitched and went still. It was as though a curtain had been drawn across the man's eyes. Holman knew Cash

Anders was dead.

He swore under his breath.

More gunfire. The rifle over at the cabin was probing for him again, and all at once a second weapon, a handgun from the sound of it, had joined the first one. He knew then he had no choice. If he stayed where he was, between them they were certain to tag him. And he simply had to have Cash Anders's revolver.

He didn't give himself time to measure the risk. He came out from his hiding place in a single explosive lunge. As he leaped over Anders's body he bent and scooped up the gun and went on, not breaking stride. At every moment he expected to be knocked off his feet. A bullet thudded into the ground by his boot just as he set it down and he distinctly felt the jar. He took a headlong dive for the protection of a boulder and made it, not quite believing he was still alive.

A bullet followed him in, screaming off the boulder's face. Holman let impetus carry him rolling on up to his knees, the gun rising in his fist. Over in front of the cabin, he saw that Sid Flagg had joined Griffin, limping, with one leg of his trousers cut away and a bandage tied around his thigh. He was running recklessly forward in his eagerness to get another shot at Holman.

Mouth grim, the latter triggered a bullet and caught him. Flagg was flung spinning, and

Holman dropped before Luke Griffin's rifle could target him. When he looked again, Griffin was no longer in sight.

Griffin would have taken his warning from what happened to Flagg and withdrawn into the cabin, when he saw that his enemy had reached cover and now possessed a gun. Flagg lay where he had fallen, and Travis Holman paid him no further attention. He had killed enough men so he knew what a dead one looked like.

With the sudden pause in the gunfire and the ebbing of the last echoes bouncing against the high walls surrounding the cup, stillness settled again. Holman took the moment to check the gun he had snatched from under its dead owner's hand, saw with a grimace that it was a different caliber from the shells in his own belt. It left him with four usable bullets. Rocking the cylinder back into place, he set the hammer on an unexploded shell and weighted the revolver in his palm while he considered the silent cabin.

No movement there and no sign of Luke Griffin, who might be inside but perhaps had already left by another door or window, invisible from this point. He even now might be stalking Holman, maneuvering to get at him from an unsuspected quarter. Meanwhile the seconds were ticking by, and waiting could wear on a man's nerves. Holman decided he must carry the fight to his enemy.

He broke from cover and made a quick, prowling run to his right, keeping low and taking what advantage he could of the terrain that lay between him and the nearer of the two corrals. He expected to draw fire but still the silence held, drawing out painfully, stretching his nerves. In a last burst he cut across an open space and flung himself behind a corner post and held tight there while he studied the blind side of the shack.

There was nothing—only the uneasy stirring of the mules that circled the pole enclosure, moving away from him, their hoofs kicking up a urine stink from the torn and muddy earth. Holman put his left side to the pen and started along it, moving fast now. He rounded a turn, trailed the corral's length to the corner nearest the cabin. The wall that faced him had no opening. Quickly he crossed to it, pressed his shoulders to the logs and held there a moment trying to control the sound of his own breathing.

Luke Griffin might be anywhere. The very next step Holman took might lead him into the sights of the rifle that had already killed Cash Anders.

The sweat was beginning to trickle under his shirt as he turned toward the cabin's rear. At the corner he hesitated, again listening. There was still no sound from Griffin, though a jay suddenly exploded with raucous cries from a pine tree crown in the timber some hundred yards to his right. Tensed, he jerked about to watch it fly off across the rim, its racket fading. He decided finally it could not have been Luke Griffin who startled the bird, if in fact anything had.

So, turning back, he slid around the corner. The shack did indeed have an open rear window. Luke Griffin stood with his shoulders against the logs just this side of it, not a dozen feet from Holman.

Rifle held in one hand, Griffin was peering up the lift of the rock slope, hunting, perhaps, a good place to hole up and wait for Holman to enter his sights. For a slow count of three, neither man made a move. Then something seen out of the tail of his eye must have warned the outlaw. His head jerked about, and his eyes met Holman's.

The latter said, 'I can kill you before you raise the rifle, Luke. Throw it down.'

Those other eyes burned at him. The lips moved on unspoken, furious words. And then, plainly, Holman saw the man's intention reflected even before he moved. The rifle's barrel tipped up. It was a clumsy and desperate effort. With his six-shooter already leveled, Holman could have killed the outlaw instantly. Still he held off the trigger, hoping the man would think better of what he was doing. At the last instant, with the black muzzle lining on his chest, there was no choice left. He shifted his aim slightly, just before he fired, trying for a crippling shot that would stop Griffin without killing him.

As fate would have it, Griffin chose just then to lunge aside—straight into the bullet's path. It took him dead center. As he went back and down, striking the logs, the rifle in his hand sent a shot screeching blindly overhead.

Travis Holman lowered the smoking revolver and dragged a palm across his mouth. A pulsing of echoes died against the rock lifts; silence returned. Reluctantly he prodded his fallen enemy with a toe, and felt the dead give of the lifeless body.

The curious relationship between them had begun in a side street in Santa Fe; it had ended here. He drew a ragged breath, and slid the gun into its holster as he lifted his head and looked up the rock slope toward the old mine adit, just above him.

It was going to be a sizable chore, to dig those shipments of stolen bullion out of there, load them on those mules by himself, and return them to Rincon with the bodies of the men who had been killed here. He might as well be getting at it.

* * *

Omar Talbert peered at the tall, tired man through the upper section of his bifocals. 'Shattuck?' the doctor repeated. 'Oh, he's all right. I patched him up and sent him home.

Our deputy sheriff will survive.'

'What about Chess?' Holman demanded.

'He needed more work. But I got the bullet out, and right now he's in my back room, under surveillance. I'll have to keep him there a while.'

'But he'll live?' And at the little man's nod: 'Could I see him long enough to give him some news?'

The other hesitated, fingering his white goatee. 'Is it good news?'

'The best!'

'It might help him. Go ahead.' The doctor stood aside for him. 'But you'd better make it brief.'

Holman nodded, and went through the office to the inner door and opened it on a room that had been painted white, and fitted out with a couple of iron beds. In one of these, Frank Chess lay upon his back, his eyes closed, slow and steady breathing lifting the sheet above his bandaged chest. Holman hesitated, at sight of Allie Baker seated by the bed. As she looked up he went in, pulling off his hat. 'Is he asleep?'

She shook her head. 'I don't think so.' Her eyes showed she had a hundred questions to ask, but Holman turned away to lay a hand on the hurt man's shoulder. He had to speak his name twice before Frank Chess opened his eyes.

'Holman!' he exclaimed. 'You got back!

What happened after—?'

'You'll hear it all,' Holman told him. 'For now, the only thing you need to know is that the gold's been recovered.'

Allie Baker stared. Chess, himself, seemed unable to understand at first. '*All* of it?' he stammered.

'Every bar. I've just been down to the freight office, and turned it over to Burl Dempster. So relax, and get well. You're out of the woods.'

Disbelief struggled with joy, and with the sedative that dulled the hurt man's eyes. 'If it's really true,' he murmured finally, moving his head on the pillow, 'what can I say? Except—thanks!'

A shade embarrassed, Holman answered, 'I was paid to do a job. Now I can go report to Sam Mayberly that his bank's investment is safe.'

Closing the door again behind him, he nodded to Talbert and went through the office to stand a moment staring out into the street. He felt a deep weariness, and something else, a weight of emotion that he couldn't precisely define until, as he stood there, he heard that other door open again. Allie Baker's quick steps crossed the office toward him. He turned slowly to face her.

'It's really true?' she exclaimed, her brown eyes searching his face. 'You actually did it? And single-handed?'

'It was my job to do,' he said again.

'And now—you talk as though you're leaving.'

He looked at her steadily. 'Is there any reason I shouldn't?' he asked finally, and saw his answer in the way she lowered her eyes from his gaze. 'It's still Chess, isn't it?' he demanded. 'You've made your pick?'

Her head lifted. She put out a hand and found his own. 'I hope you see. I love him. I can't change that.'

'No,' he agreed. He saw a great deal more, in that moment, that he had tried not to admit to himself. Like the fact that he had nothing to offer such a girl as this, that his way of life held no place for her. There was no pleasure in such knowledge, but facts were meant to be faced.

'You better go back to him now,' Travis Holman said gruffly. She nodded and squeezed his hand and suddenly stepped close to kiss him on the cheek. After that she turned again to the other room, where Omar Talbert stood beside his patient's bed.

Not looking after her, Travis Holman swung away and stepped into the glow of late afternoon. He had to pull on his hat and drag it low, to shade his oddly smarting eyes as the sun's level rays stabbed into them.

We hope you have enjoyed this Large Print book. Other Chivers Press or G.K. Hall & Co. Large Print books are available at your library or directly from the publishers.

For more information about current and forthcoming titles, please call or write, without obligation, to:

Chivers Press Limited
Windsor Bridge Road
Bath BA2 3AX
England
Tel. (01225) 335336

OR

Thorndike Press
295 Kennedy Memorial Drive
Waterville
Maine 04901
USA

All our Large Print titles are designed for easy reading, and all our books are made to last.